CONIUM REVIEW

vol. 8

Conium Press
Portland, OR

The Conium Review
Vol. 8

Portland, OR

http://www.coniumreview.com

ISBN-13 978-1-942387-15-2
ISSN 2164-6252

Cover Image: © spxChrome / iStock
Layout & Design: James R. Gapinski

THE CONIUM REVIEW
vol. 8

James R. Gapinski
Managing Editor

Sarah Gerard
Contest Judge

[contents]

[contents]

THREE RIFFS FOR THE DEVIL

INNOVATIVE SHORT FICTION CONTEST WINNER

Joe Aguirre

THREE RIFFS FOR THE DEVIL

INNOVATIVE SHORT FICTION CONTEST WINNER

Joe Aguirre

I. The True Christ

Once in every lifetime, the Devil appears enfleshed, touting his dark buffet of sweet temptations. For most of us, the Devil appears as a mortal enemy, a worst nightmare, or the classic dapper gentleman. To certain rare saints, however, he appears disguised as Christ. In this latter form, the Devil tempted the mystic anchorite Blessed Severin of Pamphylia.

On his day of temptation, Severin sat praying in his mud-walled cell under a solitary hill in the center of a salt flat. Eighty-eight years prior, he'd bricked himself in. As a boy, Severin lived on this flat, which was then a prairie. Around his childhood village, plagues spread, armies clashed, and those fiefholders with legal title to God's material universe started brushfires just to hassle one another's livestock enterprises. Severin's classmates succumbed young to the plagues or wars or else lived to bond into some noble's perpetual servitude. Severin chose underground hermitage.

Above his cell, politics happened. Villagers dwindled, fiefdoms relocated to prairies in more favorable tax jurisdictions, and fires stripped the foliage. Alone below,

Severin prayed night and day that children, soldiers, and nobility alike might live humbly. By the Lord's command, he fasted, eating only enough proteinaceous grubs and lichens necessary to sustain his prayers. Severin prayed faithfully, but Christ sent no feedback on whether these prayers mattered. Severin knew this was part of the test. Still, he hoped ever in his heart for some tangible, miraculous sign.

So the Devil shows up wearing the robe, beard, and ratty sandals of Christ. As he passes through the wall of Severin's cell, he bumps into the True Christ, arriving by heavenly coincidence to bring Severin a prophecy.

"My Lord and—my Lord!" Severin prostrates himself uncertainly before the identical Christs.

"Severin," calls the True Christ. "Carry my word to the people of the City!"

"No, good and faithful Severin!" the Devil beckons. "This prophecy is false. Come instead to your eternal reward!"

Severin begins to weep. "All my life I wished to glimpse you. Now, your appearance shakes my faith! Some sign, Lord, of your will?"

"No sign," chides the True Christ. "I ask faithfulness, regardless of signs."

"What he said," says the Devil.

The True Christ lifts Severin to his feet. "Severin, misconceptions abound about me. People say I don't dish more than anyone can handle, but you know that's untrue. People say there's blessing hidden in all I mete and dole, but that's at best a gross oversimplification. Suffering is a problem, but be patient. To get to the world without it, surrender your will. In my experience, the way to do that is to pitch into a stack of work, or in your case, deliver this holy prophecy."

The Devil interrupts. "Severin, temptation takes many forms: temptations of power, temptations of lust, but also temptations of false martyrdom. You *are* holy, possibly the holiest being in creation. Is that not enough? Tell me, do you want to bring this prophecy as a servant, or as a *savior*?" He leans in closer. "Severin, would you usurp my place?"

Severin considers both Christs, then closes his eyes. Long he contemplates, so long that fresh lichens bloom across the walls before he's finished. When he finally opens his eyes, though, his countenance radiates. "My Lord, you know my innermost heart. If pride hides within my best intention, you shall forgive. My only conscious want is to do your will. Your prophecy, my Lord."

The True Christ smiles upon Severin.

"Fine, enjoy more earthly suffering!" The Devil doesn't normally show mortals his powers, but because he's pissed, he brandishes his pointy tail and blasts the cell apart. With a sound like popcorn, he turns the fifty closest boulders into buns of steaming pumpernickel, then rockets skyward in a sulfurous whoosh.

He's miffed he didn't get that soul, but as he soars above burning prairies, blighted cities, and starving babies with bellies like balloons, he is somewhat comforted.

Severin must go tell the Citizens, whose current fad is a lamb's blood cleanse, to desist or else face asteroids. The Lord outlines talking points, then ascends to celestial flutes, lutes, and sunshowers. Severin sees, shimmering far across the salt flats, the City's exurban developments, and nearer, the Devil's bread turning to sand.

Post-temptation, Severin feels relieved but peckish. He notices that one stray bun hasn't dematerialized.

The Lord commandeth fasting, but before Severin's right hand's the wiser, his left hand gouges a good-sized pumpernickel chunk. The bread, sweet and spongy, goes straight to his soul. He will hike to the City, Severin decides, once this meal is finished. Out of the sand behind Severin, with pats of butter melting in their cross-creased crowns, two more buns appear.

II. Phantom Hands are the Devil's Playthings

Garth Graves, guitarist, jammed passably as a kid, back when knowing the riffs from "Raining Blood" or "Symphony of Destruction" meant something, but then he stood for years, decades, behind a Guitar Center register, too deep in Klonopin and daydreams to practice chromatic scales. He never made practice a habit, but his other habits progressed quickly. One moment he was slouching behind that register, the next he was pawning his Ronnie James Dio Edition Flying V for cheap gak. Now he's floundering, moments from overdose, staring from a motel bathtub into the Devil's eyes.

The Devil appears to Garth in a gaucho hat, mariachi jacket, and chaps the color of midnight.

"Who the hell are you supposed to be?" Garth asks.

The Devil sighs. "You worshipped me once."

"If you're the devil," Garth sputters, "how come you look like a classic rock douche?"

The Devil doesn't normally do this, but because he's pissed, he splits the floor and flashes Garth a glimpse of damned souls stoking Hell's sooty boilers.

"Garth, I'm the guy who'll become the world's greatest player now that *you* never will." As proof, the Devil plucks a nylon stringed guitar out of the air and rips a few suave bars of "Nuages."

Garth pounds the tile wall. "Damnit! If I'd only had more time."

"Time's up," the Devil coos. "Unless—"

"Unless?"

"You give me your soul."

"No more life," Garth wails. "Unless it's as the greatest."

Whatever. I'll make you the greatest. But I'll need your soul *plus* something extra. What giveth thee, Garth?"

"Umm—" Garth blurts his first idea. "My right arm."

The Devil cocks an eyebrow. "'Arm?' Don't you need that?"

"Please. Greatest. Guitar," Garth gurgles, losing consciousness.

The Devil shrugs, then vanishes with a whipcrack and a belch of smoke.

When he wakes, dressed, atop his motel bed, Garth's right shoulder is a clean stump without blood or scars. His shirtsleeve hangs like a limp windsock. His pockets hold rolled, vaguely sulfurous twenties, enough to redeem a Ronnie James Dio Edition Flying V.

"You got my guitar?" Garth asks the pawnbroker.

"You got money? Jesus, what happened to your—"

Garth slaps down bills. "Bring it."

"But you can't possibly—"

"There's a strap. Put it on me. Put it on me!" Garth shrieks, his voice reaching demonic pitches.

Wearing the guitar, Garth feels peculiar wholeness, like the first moment after a migraine. He raises his left hand to the neck. The moment his fingers touch string, they begin pistoning up and down. His single hand solos, hammering notes clearer than picked ones. The guitar's brassy unpredictable tones come like tremors announcing vengeful sandworms tunneling from below.

The pawnbroker wipes away tears. "Holy hell, Garth, you're the greatest."

Garth's rise is like all the biopics: long limos, thrashing fans, daps from Steve Vai, Joe Satriani, and John Petrucci—even Buckethead gives him a nod from beneath his bucket. Garth leaves a gold-plated Garth Graves Edition Flying V at the tomb of Ronnie James Dio. He's set to continue soloing into the annals of history, until an ascendant blogger points something out. "Garth looks ridiculous!" She couches this in a thinkpiece positing that all guitar solos are rockist macho ridiculousness, so she is not labeled ableist. The thought enters everyone's head, "Garth looks ludicrous!" Strutting onstage, his one arm noodling back and forth, whiddly-doo-dee! Whenever he plays, people laugh, and Garth's mystique evaporates.

Garth, soused, confronts the journalist at some industry fete. "Who lets you cut me down with one stupid blurb?"

She smirks. "Me? The greatest alternative music journalist of all time? Nobody—." By the flicker in her eye, it's clear she's made her own bargain.

Garth becomes a punchline. People boost status within their friend groups by zinging him. After another hostile concert, some punk with a septum bar offers to shake Garth's hand. Garth reaches out, but the kid pulls his hand back.

"Whoa, wait, you jack off with that one, right?" The punk's punk friends fall out cackling.

"I don't have time to jack off," Garth stammers. "Too busy playing the world's greatest riffs."

From their laughter, though, he knows he sounds

flustered, so he chokes the kid with devilstrength, chokes him dead.

They won't give Garth a guitar for jailhouse blues, but prison is otherwise fine. The gangs are low key, Garth's celly is chill, and the state has a robust anti-rape initiative. They take classes, therapize in chair circles, and even scare whole classes of visiting middle schoolers straight, but none of it feels like the life the Devil promised. Garth mopes around the yard, choking up on an invisible neck, replaying his part over and over and over—.

III. A Pure Soul

The Devil comes one night for Jenni as her ex-husband Earle.

Jenni sits on her couch in a halo of lamplight, painting her toes like ladybugs, when the Devil knocks.

"Open up," he calls. Jenni hears Earle's voice and scampers for the kitchen drawer.

"Open up!"

Jenni does. Eyes covered, she sticks her arm through the cracked door and fires fifteen wild rounds. The bullets pass right through the Devil's chest. When the Devil shoulders open the door and knocks her down, Jenni assumes she missed.

She clutches her bathrobe close. "What do you want?"

"Not much." The Devil steps across the threshold. "Just your soul."

"When you left you called me a soulless bitch," Jenni sobs, scooting back into the lamplight by the couch.

"That wasn't me," the Devil chuckles. "That was your ex-husband Earle."

Jenni snorts. "You here to tell me you a changed man,

Earle? Please."

"I'm not Earle. I'm the Devil."

"And the Antichrist too?" Earle used to play this game when she was stoned. "Enough, Earle. Get gone."

"Not until you hear my deal."

Jenni sighs, arms crossed. "Whatever, Earle."

"Jenni, I can give you a body that shimmers like the Northern Lights are just beneath your skin. I can give you the voice of a young Tammy Wynette, never-ending credit cards, or the power to talk to dogs. Anything. Everything. All I ask in return is your soul."

For a long moment, Jenni says nothing. Then, she laughs. "Earle, when you left me, you left bills, garbage, and those goddamn busted jet skis you stole from Christ knows where. The only men who called round then was repo men. Now, I got a shift at Waffle House, I'm paying down these loans, and three nights a week, I wash dogs at the shelter. I got three months now, and Momma lets me pick her up and take her to church. After, we get Blizzards. It ain't much, Earle, but it's my life, and I wouldn't want your fancy promises even if they was true." She pats the Devil's arm. "And Earle? These days I'm strong enough to *pray* for you. Now get moving."

The touch of a pure soul! It burns like ice. The Devil flings off her hand. He doesn't normally do this, but because he's pissed, he opens his palm and flicks up a little ball of hellfire, just for a second, like his hand is a lighter. Jenni falls dazed onto the couch.

"I told you, I'm the goddamn Devil! I show up as your enemy, nightmare, whatever—Jenni, this is how I work!"

Jenni digests this. "So, this happens at lot, probably—you appearing as people's exes."

Now the Devil digests. "Actually—no. Never." He

grows wistful. "Look, everybody thinks their ex is the worst person in the world, but believe me, they aren't, not even the worst person out there for them. If people thought back, they'd find some good times, passion, real fire even—" Then he shudders. "Earle excepted, of course."

Jenni giggles. The Devil wears his Wranglers better than Earle did, though his have the same nasty Skoal ring she always dogged Earle about. She adjusts her hair.

"You said 'talk to dogs?'" Jenni asks. The bathrobe jostles just a smidgen down.

"I did." The Devil looks her over. "So how about that soul?" He floats on a cloud of sulfur to the vacant part of the couch.

"My God—you look like Earle though," Jenni murmurs, but she leans into his toasty body and nuzzles his neck. Beneath the sulfur musk, his skin smells like cinnamon and scorched marshmallows.

"Why the hell not?" she says and cuts the lamplight.

COLORLESS

Jenny Wu

COLORLESS

Jenny Wu

On the morning that the chairman's death was announced, an old photograph of my father, "the general," pictured beside him—the two smiling at one another, the chairman in his star-cap, the general in his furs, their eyes like half-moons—resurfaced on the floor of the bookstore.

Three hundred thousand copies, to be exact, had been dropped off at the bookstore, sometime between the hours of three and five. At the nearby press, this same photograph, along with quotations from my father's speeches, spliced together and out of context, snuck in between the regular broadsides. Back then the bookstore had only one twittering staircase. The morning clerks, scrambling to sweep up the mess before the day's first crowds, were among those who denounced the perpetrator.

Some say my father was the chairman's friend; some say he'd been plotting against the chairman since his days in the army. Hearing apocryphal tales, seeing downright doctored photographs, I'm used to by now. I spent many evenings cross-legged on the floor of my boyfriend's sparsely furnished apartment, smoking hand-rolled cigarettes, listening to his theories of how my father died.

My father left me few writings and passed through a life of civil service with neither charisma nor a unique philosophical view. According to the blueprints of my father's botched coup, my father was to personally stalk and intercept the chairman, coded "M." in his plan, on his way from the capital to the XX villa, and challenge him in his private train car to a face-to-face pistol duel.

The thought of such a duel makes me laugh. The chairman never took the train he was scheduled for, and he never sat in the car he was given. It would have been impossible to find him on a train, much less kill him. But at the height of the frenzy, while the police were busy fanning the apocryphal flame of my father's betrayal—for he was lumped in with several other criminals—my boyfriend became obsessed. He believed if he could work out the inner logic of the thing, he could prove to me the veracity of the claims. At that time, I'd been out of prison for two years, and I had, or so I thought, successfully assumed the identity of an anonymous factory worker, but then as soon as I came through the door, it didn't matter that I was still in my uniform from the automotive plant, or that I was nauseated from the crowded evening bus, he'd be right at it, talking about the blueprints again.

Supposed coup aside, my father's political plans had already begun to backfire. At the time, according to his one diary, he'd been purifying the army in anticipation of an invasion that may or may not have been his own invention, and he'd been doing so at the expense of the chairman's second-in-command. I hadn't known. All I knew was that my family's airplane had crashed in the mountains, on its way out of the country.

They say that, when asked if my father should die, the chairman had answered with a proverb: "The sky will rain. The widowed mother will remarry. Let it be." I think of that proverb when it rains, and it makes me itch.

For one, the authorities were unable to prove that my father was aboard the aircraft. Often, someone told me, bodies in these types of accidents are scattered like sand, or they're burnt, along with their forged dossiers and sleeping pill prescriptions, beyond recognition. In this case, they explained, my father's DNA would have resembled too closely that of my family members nearby to know for sure. Then the police went to the crash site and searched for his teeth.

I was with my father on the night before his death. Although the official report states that my father was in the capital with the chairman, I know that my father was with us at the XX villa, on the seacoast, where our family and other political families used to holiday, where I personally hung scarecrows and lit lanterns along the pier that snaked into the sea. The three of them planned to leave the country in the morning. Whether my father was going to seek asylum after the failed assassination I do not know; of the family, I knew the least at all times. I spent a sleepless night walking up and down the pier, fingering my father's diary in my pocket, then telephoned the chairman's second-in-command, my father's closest ally. I told him my brother was planning to force our father into something against his will. In prison they laughed at me—how could I be so stupid? That man was my father's enemy.

. . .

I am presently traveling by train. Beside me are two wine glasses rattling against each other on an idle cart, like teeth searching for warmth. I am looking now at new, never-before-seen photographs of my parents in a foreign newspaper. Only two, though—none of my young, inept brother.

The first photograph is of my mother, her skull round and toothy and hairless. My father's the police boiled in a pot of water, to remove the skin and hair; here it looks like a stitched-up egg. This is news to me too! I throw my head back and laugh because I can—no one on this train knows who I am.

Some said that during my three-year prison sentence I tried to commit suicide. That is untrue. Instead I had a game going with the guards. A betting game, in which the wager was my body. "You fought them?" an old friend asks.

"Life before prison was the same game," I say. I refuse to explain any further.

"You chose to bet because you wanted to at least hit them, didn't you?" the old friend presses me. "You wanted to scare them, make them see you as some crazy woman rolling in hay, didn't you?"

I keep on me a few photographs, some from my early years, some from before my birth. The four of us, a white cloth hung behind us, my brother and me on our father's left and right knee, respectively, my mother slightly apart. Lately, an old friend sent to pay me a visit saw my parents' wedding photograph and said, smiling through his set of yellow teeth, "You have a beautiful son."

I remember my father having to attend a meeting, phoning in an order at a restaurant for my mother, my brother, and me ahead of time. Sitting at the table watching plate after plate come out. No sooner had the waitress come with a platter of steamed fish, than she came again with a plate of bean curd. We told the waitress to stop the order; the plates were stacked like pyramids, covering every centimeter of the tablecloth and more. She said, "Oh, that was the last dish." The other waitresses eyed us judgmentally. Class difference in a classless society. My mother, a politician in her own right, a member of the chairman's outer circle, refused to eat anything, told me to stop eating. This was her form of protest. But, lest I further offend the waitresses, I ate until I was bursting. My brother, too, but for different reasons no doubt, kept shoveling food into his mouth. Then the three of us reunited with my father in a private car, in which my mother said nothing to my father save for "Watch yourself." Because the order was not for us; it was for show.

I remember meetings of free-thinkers in a small room at night, one yellow lightbulb. They didn't want their photos taken. The light was an antique yellow. A vague buzzing unsettled the air by the papered casement window, threatening to envelope the compound, and the debaters' light was flickering as though it wanted to be the source of the sound—a giant yellow insect.

A photo of someone's child—my father—standing in the rubble of a street, looking like the subject of a foreign photographer. The child's pants were pulled up past his navel, making his legs look as long as a locust's. But there hadn't been a bombing.

"No, they lived there," my mother said, rubbing her thumb over the building in the background.

What I remember of my father, his presence, amounts to nothing: intimate absurdities—personal drivel, like watching him squat on the toilet. I remember he had neurasthenia, and a bullet wound in his skull, both of which flared up when he got near the ocean. I remember once, at the XX villa, he was washing his feet, sitting cross-legged on his daybed and drying his feet one by one with a face towel. He said he needed help clipping his toenails, he had a pair of small scissors on the bamboo mat; I refused and told a maid to do it. Later I passed by my brother on the veranda, and he snickered, "Father says you clip his toenails. How pious of you." As he turned to go, I suddenly remembered a time, as a young girl, I rode on my father's back, and sometime afterwards he clipped my toenails, and fingernails, gathering the sharp little moons into his big palm. He had done so without resentment.

▪ ▪ ▪

The chairman fell to Parkinson's disease, his vision clouded over with cataracts, in his private residence. He and my father died in the same week in September, five years apart. On the anniversary of my father's death, I got to enjoy the sight of people parading through the streets, crying into handkerchiefs. A belated parade in my father's honor. The people were afraid that, if they did not cry, they would be spotted and punished. They were following orders out of fear, and later they would be said to have been brainwashed. But I have no need to hide or fake. The chairman had been the one who personally ordered my release from prison. Someone new succeeded him. We'd all believed my father would. Secretly, my brother had placed himself next in line.

A different rumor, started perhaps by loyal apologists, circulated, claiming that my brother had kidnapped my father and forced his hand. Of course, the word "kidnapped" is so vague. These people said they saw my brother, in a panic, boarding the aircraft at dawn and that it was my brother, alone, who died over the mountains. Yet others said that my brother was being manipulated by someone else who had it out for my father, but there was no evidence in support of this claim. They all knew that my brother ran a sex shop as a means of amassing an entourage of loyal clients, political wannabes, to serve him once he succeeded my father. They said it was garish inside.

Even my boyfriend was convinced that the strategist had blundered—that, in framing my father, his political enemies underestimated the resources he had had at his disposal. Though this was his first theory, my boyfriend was just as easily won over by rhetoric, and he shifted his suspicions onto my brother. I said nothing; I let the smoke coil out of my mouth, out the open window, to join the air inside the steam-cooker of the city and the laundry on the adjacent apartments that quivered in the heat. Meanwhile, my boyfriend raved, my father had drafted an even more meticulous and astonishing plan, one that would send the chairman rushing into his mountainside bunker on the northern border and there gas him to death.

In this particular re-staging, the chairman discovered my father's plan ahead of time, and, after calculating everything perfectly, invited my parents to dinner at his private residence, where my father sat colorlessly while being entertained with perhaps a dish of rustic bean curd, perhaps a mysterious folk dancer, perhaps a man with a sparrow-like voice, and then sent my parents off in their private car, to careen down the macadam road, accompanied overhead by one barely perceptible rocket curving into the night, falling ever closer, ever closer.

I've come to accept that a poisonous indigestion of paranoia, fear, and his own self-consciousness lay at the root of my boyfriend's obsession. I realized this when he ran away, as most people back then seemed to be doing, in one way or another.

. . .

On the night before my family disappeared, I saw my young, inept brother crouched and facing the sea, the sky behind him dark and gray, his soft hair buoyant in the wind, up to his usual tricks, holding a seabird by a rope, flying it like a noisy kite. He looked up at me with innocent eyes and said "I thought you'd gone to sleep."

I see my face in the train window. My brother—only twenty-six when he died. Prickly landscapes, whole villages, rush by, giving way to the furrowed hillsides, a maze of water-green leaves and carved paths. There is little political color left in my cheeks. I am tired now.

CHALLENGER

Debbie Graber

CHALLENGER

Debbie Graber

Common traits of high school reunion organizers:

1. Overachievers.

2. Popular in high school.

3. Motivated to see people from high school at least once a decade.

4. Assess themselves as leaders.

5. Enjoy event planning.

6. Seek reminders of a time when things seemed easier.

7. Consider high school the best time of their lives.

8. Excel at selectively forgetting the bad things they did and said in high school.

9. Need to demonstrate to their former classmates how awesome they are.

. . .

Hackneys Pub was a no-brainer as the venue for the reunion. It was local, had been around forever, and the Shillelagh Room downstairs easily accommodated up to two-hundred-twenty people for a cocktail reception. Everyone would appreciate the passed appetizers of sliders on dark bread and a fried up mound of onion straws referred to by regulars as "cat gut." And the catering manager offered to throw in either a stationary cheese platter or an onion dip fountain, depending on availability.

Another plus was that The Shillelagh Room had room for three hosted bars. The former Titans would want to get their drinks quickly to take the nervous edge off, even the ones who swore off partying after a fatty liver scare. The organizers didn't want to read on Facebook afterwards that it took forever to get the "Titanini," the reunion signature drink made with vodka and elderflower liqueur. That sort of thing would reflect badly on their planning skills, and they couldn't live with themselves if that happened.

John Anastas was the lead organizer. He lived in London, but he was able to do most of the planning using social media. He only leaned on the local committee when necessary. This was surprising since John was known at his workplace for being a micromanager. As a Marketing Vice-President for Shazam, John did the tasks of his subordinates when he should have delegated. He was a laughing stock amongst the other executives. While most of them showed up to work around ten, John started his day in the office at six thirty. You could trace this type of behavior back to high school, when John was a member of every high school club, except for the debate team, which was too nerdy for his image.

Generally speaking, John didn't have a ton of patience. John would say "You're taking too long ordering from Just Eats," grabbing his boyfriend Matthias's phone away from him. "I thought you millennials grew up on technology." Matthias would chuckle, swirling his glass of bourbon before taking a long, deep swig. But if John looked at Matthias's chiseled face more closely, he would have noticed a certain hardness there, if he were sensitive to that kind of thing. But John was not that kind of reunion organizer.

The local reunion committee was made up of good planners. Laurie Peel in particular did a terrific job making decorations for the reunion. She and co-committee member Gretchen Stillman kept their photos from high school, which Laurie copied to use in detailed shoebox dioramas. John was grateful they had taken this project on with little direction. He considered it a major "win."

> 10. Reunion organizers obsessively count their accomplishments, even if a "win" involves a glue gun.

Laurie never considered herself a crafty person, but she really enjoyed the reunion projects. She became engrossed in her work on the dioramas, fastidiously gluing photo heads onto tiny doll bodies and bedazzling their outfits with Titan green and gold sequins until she noticed that three hours had gone by. Laurie began to understand a little about creativity and mindfulness. She even considered taking a University of Chicago Extension class in printmaking. But then things got busy: her son needed tutoring in algebra, and her daughter was going through a rough puberty, and Laurie told herself she didn't have time for personal growth. But the truth was that she'd never been comfortable trying new things and especially driving to places she'd never been to before. Her chest tightened thinking about where she would park. She was also fearful about the other people who would take the class: There could be people from "fringe" neighborhoods; people who spray-painted graffiti art on underpasses. People with tattoos on their faces. What would they make of her, a Subaru mom from the northwest suburbs? It was easy to talk herself out of it.

> 11. Reunion organizers don't stray far from their comfort zone.
>
> 12. Reunion organizers maintain the status quo.

John and Laurie and Gretchen were friends in high school. Meredith Tandy, the last member to join the committee, was not part of their social circle. Meredith was one of the class scapegoats. Senior year, Meredith was nominated for Homecoming Queen as a joke. The dean of students knew her nomination was a put on—Meredith was skinny, wore thick glasses and didn't seem to have any friends, but he felt that the rules should be followed. This was the eighties, after all, and no one cared much about bullied kids, except for the bullied kids themselves.

The other Homecoming Queen nominees that year

were student council president Petra Mullaly and Lissa Powers, who rumor had it, had been approached to model for *Seventeen Magazine*.

As a nominee, Meredith was required to attend the dance and stand up on stage with all the other nominees and a date (her brother). The Titans booed when her name was read, and cheered loudly when Petra Mullaly and Fred Freitag were crowned queen and king. Most reunion organizers can recall their humiliating high school experiences because there weren't that many to remember. Once in a while though, a reunion organizer's four years of high school were a digest of humiliating experiences that can never be forgotten, no matter how much therapy she might have.

John wasn't sure what to say when Meredith messaged him on Twitter about joining the committee. He would have felt more comfortable with someone else, but neither Lissa Powers nor Petra Mullaly nor Fred Freitag for that matter had replied to his Facebook messages about the reunion. He ran it by Laurie and Gretchen, and they were both fine with Meredith. They had come to realize that bullying in any form was wrong. Gretchen recently took away her daughter's phone as punishment when she saw she had retweeted, "#oliviamacnaryisanuglycrier," about a girl from her sixth grade class.

Gretchen did not remember this, but at the beginning of junior year, she stole Meredith Tandy's bra from a gym locker. It was one of those humid midwestern days in September, so Meredith was forced to finish out the school day braless and without the benefit of a light sweater to cover herself up with. And not one of the Phys Ed teachers even thought to offer Meredith a sweatshirt. This was the eighties, after all, and the Phys Ed teachers were too busy sniffing coke in the teachers lounge to give a rat's ass about Meredith's missing bra.

Gretchen also forgot that Fred Freitag gave Meredith a titty twister during lunch that day in front of everyone in the cafeteria. Even the burnouts sitting on the burnout bench came running down the hall to watch.

> 13. Reunion organizers would like to believe they were nice to everyone in high school, but they are kidding themselves.

The committee held their first meeting on Skype several months before the reunion. Because of the time difference in the UK, John was already at home after work, drinking his second glass of wine. The others were getting ready for their days: Gretchen had opened a yoga studio in Wilmette, just a few miles from where she had grown up. Laurie and her family lived in nearby Morton Grove, not far from Maiers Bakery, where most moms got their kids' birthday cakes. No one knew where Meredith Tandy lived.

Growing up, Meredith's family didn't have the money to spend on cakes from Maiers Bakery. For birthdays, Meredith's mom would make yellow Duncan Hines cakes with frosting from a can. Meredith and her brother thought their mom's birthday cakes were the greatest, but it was only because they had nothing to compare her cake against, because they were never invited to any kids' birthday parties.

If Fred Freitag had attended any of Meredith's birthday parties, which consisted of Meredith and her brother, he would have said, "This cake tastes like dog shit." And he wouldn't have been exactly wrong. Mrs. Tandy's cakes could sometimes taste like Palmolive, if she hadn't had time to wash out her mixing bowl completely.

Fred Freitag's mom was one of Maiers Bakery's best customers, buying a dozen cinnamon rolls every week to bring to her bridge club. Sometimes, she bought an extra strawberry whipped cream cake to eat by herself in the afternoon.

. . .

John called Laurie and Gretchen a few minutes early on Skype so they could catch up before they got Meredith on the line. John worried it would come across as disrespectful to talk about their mutual friends in front of her. In the eighties, they wouldn't have even thought twice about it, but their consciousness had been raised in many ways since then.

Even though they were high school friends, John never mentioned to Gretchen and Laurie that he had come out as a gay man. He didn't think it was necessary. He talked about his life and relationships openly. Things had changed a lot for John since high school: he had majored in business and moved to London for work, where he met Matthias, a freelance editor; the two of them had the opportunity and finances to travel to fascinating places whenever they could; John was done caring about what anyone thought of his lifestyle.

> 14. A reunion organizer may think he's evolved to a place where he is done caring about what anyone thinks of his lifestyle, but he requires half a bottle of Cabernet before Skyping with high

school friends.

Everyone chatted for a few minutes, and then John said, "Let's call Meredith." John clicked on Meredith's number, and her face appeared on screen. She looked older than the others felt they looked. John was particularly well preserved—he worked out religiously, and he ate gluten- and dairy-free most of the time. Since Matthias was over a decade younger, John made it his personal mission to look good. He didn't want anyone thinking he was Matthias's sugar daddy. Or, god forbid, his real daddy.

Meredith's hair was pulled back into a ponytail, and even on Skype, you could see the grays sprouting out from her temples. She had deep frown lines, giving her that dreaded marionette look. Looking at Meredith on Skype reminded Laurie that she needed to schedule a Juvaderm injection. Meredith was smiling and said, "Well I'll be! Thirty years! How is it possible?" John and the others smiled back at her, a little too brightly. Then John got down to reunion business.

"We confirmed the date with Hackneys, so we're good to go there," he said.

Meredith licked her lips and said, "Mmm! I love me some of that cat gut!" Laurie and Gretchen laughed, although if you asked them why, they wouldn't have been able to explain exactly what they thought was funny.

John quickly moved on to collateral art projects, which Gretchen and Laurie offered to spearhead. Meredith said, "My dad snapped a bunch of pics at Homecoming when I was nominated for Queen, but there was a fire at their apartment a few years back and everything burned up. They lost pretty much everything, but at least everyone was okay."

Although Meredith's parents losing all their earthly possessions to a fire was horrible, the others cringed the most when she mentioned Homecoming. Her family was there taking photos, cheering her on? Did she think she had been nominated on purpose and not as a joke? Laurie cleared her throat, something she did unconsciously when she felt embarrassed.

Meredith's comment caused Gretchen to reflect upon about the fragile nature of the ego, something she hadn't thought about since her Intro to Psych class in high school. It was something Gretchen struggled with as a yoga teacher. She tried to stay present when teaching her classes, but sometimes, as she led her students through sun salutations or vinyasa flow, she would be flooded with the palpable feeling that they were judging her. As she passed by the mats, adjusting poses and offering encouragement, she could smell the sentiment hanging in the air over certain students. Usually, she could narrow down the offender, a skill she had perfected over the years. It was often someone in the back row, someone whom Gretchen didn't recognize as a regular. Usually it was a younger, aggressively toned woman—someone who looked like she had already practiced a lot of yoga in her short life. The kind of person who had attended a yoga workshop in Costa Rica, and who commemorated the experience with a colorful shoulder tattoo. Gretchen imagined her talking about the class afterwards at brunch.

"Yoga was just okay," the woman would say to her friends, "No diversity at all at that studio—just a bunch of middle-aged white women. And that teacher! The whitest woman in America! I bet her husband is a hedge fund manager and owning her own yoga studio is her 'hobby.'

She probably rides horses at her stable in the afternoon while her nanny picks the kids up from private school." Gretchen imagined the woman sipping from a bottomless mimosa in a gauzy sundress, a monarch butterfly tattoo clearly visible through the sheer fabric.

Gretchen would stop and make eye contact with this student. She would try to convey in that one glance openness and understanding, but then she would yank on the woman's rock-hard abs during the bridge pose. She would make a point to stand behind her and firmly tug her hips up a bit higher when she least expected it, like during a downward facing dog. Gretchen would experience an almost orgasmic jolt of pleasure as the student grimaced in pain.

> 15. Reunion organizers would never say the "C" word, but it's amazing how many times during yoga practice they might think it.

. . .

"Wow, that's horrible about the fire," Gretchen said. "Do you think you could research copying our senior yearbook photos for nametags?"

Meredith's brow furrowed, then smoothed out as much as it could. "It's a little tough for me because I don't have Wi-Fi. I'm at Starbucks for this call—she spun the screen around so that everyone could see the Starbucks counter and customers waiting in line. "Everyone wave! I haven't seen these people in thirty years." A few customers waved. "But no problem. I'll figure it out."

The call continued for another half-hour where they

discussed the merits of drink tickets, until Meredith said, "Oh gosh, I gotta start my shift." She stood up and the other organizers could see she was wearing a green Starbucks apron. "I'll get going on the nametags. Really exciting!" Then she hung up.

Even though it wasn't on purpose, John, Laurie, and Gretchen started laughing. If you had asked them why, they would have said it was jarring seeing Meredith after all these years. John wanted to say, "it looks like Meredith's been ridden hard," but he wasn't sure how that would land. He had taken an emotional intelligence test for work years before, and as he suspected, his numbers were through the roof. So instead he said, "She looks great for a forty-eight year-old Starbucks barista."

"She would have been voted most likely to become a barista, if we had known Starbucks was going to turn into a thing," Gretchen said.

"I bet she makes a mean pumpkin macchiato," Laurie said.

"Too bad those Homecoming photos burned up. I would love to put them in the dioramas. Talk about a time capsule," John said.

"I wouldn't be able to pick Meredith out of a lineup," Gretchen said. "It's weird how some people change so much in thirty years. I mean, I don't think I look that much different than I did in high school."

"You look practically the same!" Laurie said.

As high school kids, Laurie and Gretchen used to hang out a lot after school, mostly at Gretchen's house. Gretchen had a *Breakfast Club* poster hanging above her bed, and a Duran Duran one on the back of her door.

Laurie's parents never let her hang up anything on her bedroom walls. Her parents had put up a framed

Norman Rockwell print of a mother and father weighing their baby, and it was the only thing that remained on the wall until Laurie left for college. When she got older, if Laurie ever saw a Norman Rockwell print in a magazine or a coffee table book, she would get a horrible feeling in the pit of her stomach, which she attributed to GERD.

John didn't say it, but he did think Gretchen looked a lot different than she did in high school. He remembered Gretchen as a freckle-faced girl-next-door—slightly chubby but attractively so. Now she was very lean and her face had sharp edges with no trace of the softness she once had as a girl. John actually made out with Gretchen once in high school, after a basketball pep rally. This was back before he was willing to admit he had feelings for men, and so when he and Gretchen found themselves kissing in the parking lot, he went with it. He remembered that he fell asleep at one point during their make-out session. Looking back, it was one of the first experiences that made him think he might not be interested in women at all.

John wondered if Gretchen remembered making out with him, but there was no way he would bring it up.

16. Reunion organizers purposely avoid uncomfortable conversations.

John always had a lot of women friends, but it was Matthias who made friends easily with other men. He knew how to talk to them, how to come across confident and relaxed. He seemed so effortlessly masculine.

When John took Matthias to work functions, Matthias would laugh with the other VPs, swirling his bourbon like Dean Martin, while John stood off in the corner sulking.

17. Reunion organizers try to hide their jealous behavior but some are better at it than others.

By the end of the summer, forty-five graduates had paid the advance purchase price to attend the reunion. That number increased by thirty-two by the end of October, and then by another twenty-seven the week before the reunion. Thirty-eight more Titans bought tickets at the door. Even so, fifty more people attended the 20th reunion ten years earlier. This class had never been particularly cohesive, even in high school. They didn't have a big personality or a beloved football player holding things together, the way some other classes did. They did have Fred Freitag, who was a talented tennis player. He learned to play at his parents' country club as a kid. Fred was good-looking in a douchebaggy way, like the character Steff from *Pretty in Pink*. He partied his way through high school and a year of college at Miami of Ohio until he flunked out. When he refused to get serious about going back to school, his parents forced him to work at one of his dad's Arby's franchises. He ended up getting the cashier pregnant, and they decided to get married. After a decade, Fred's wife divorced him, and he finally hit bottom. He got sober and had a successful career as a real estate agent, specializing in the ritzy subdivisions in and around where he grew up. Fred would not attend any high school reunions on principle. He learned in recovery that he needed to avoid triggering situations that made him want to drink. He had made an inventory of the people in his life he had wronged and had directly asked them for forgiveness.

18. Fred didn't make amends to any people from high school because it was thirty years ago and he couldn't remember their names. Besides, they were all dorks anyway.

. . .

At the second Skype meeting of the reunion committee, the members talked about what to include in the last few dioramas.

"How about when the Space Shuttle Challenger blew up, and we were all watching it?" Laurie said. "I know it's sad."

Laurie still thought a lot about the Challenger accident. She remembered that a teacher, Christa Mcauliffe, had been the winner of a NASA sponsored program to be part of the crew. On the TV news conferences, she was so excited to witness all the amazing things non-astronauts would never see in their lifetimes. Laurie could imagine Christa's excitement turning to terror as the Challenger lifted off and then immediately began to break up in the atmosphere. There must have been a moment of calm in the midst of it all, Laurie thought, as the Challenger shattered into a billion fragments, and Christa and the crew became part of the mystery of space itself.

"It was impactful, definitely," John said. "But do you think we should go with something that's less of a downer? We want everyone to feel great about being at the reunion."

19. Reunion organizers learned the art

> of pivoting from their college b-school classes.

"How about a diorama with the top ten movies from 1986?" Gretchen said. "That could be fun."

"That's what I'm talking about!" John said, encouraging the narrative.

"*Pretty in Pink*—that was a good one." Meredith said. "I never saw it when it came out, but I was flipping channels a few months ago and caught it on WGN. It was amazing, even with commercials."

"Wait, you never saw *Pretty in Pink*?" Laurie said.

"We never went to the movies—we didn't have the money. Ha, who am I kidding, I don't have the money now either," Meredith laughed, although no one else did. John thought it was interesting that the Molly Ringwald character was the class pariah, just like Meredith. He wanted to press Meredith, to see if she found solace in watching Molly Ringwald deal with a lot of terrible shit from her peers but being the hero of the movie anyway.

> 20. Reunion organizers see themselves as the heroes of their own lives.

"What about the pep rallies?" Gretchen said. "The mascot doing back flips and the cheerleaders standing on each others' shoulders."

"And the variety shows," Laurie said. "Remember how the football team would do a really silly number, like they would all wear feetie pajamas and sing a song about their teddy bears?"

"Totally," Gretchen said. "I love it."

Although John attended practically every game and

variety show at the time, when pressed, he couldn't find anything he actually liked about high school. It was a difficult time for him, as he was trying to come to terms with his sexuality and get into a great college at the same time—not easy to do. But John was not about to mention that to the committee. He felt that his role in this conversation was to offer positive reinforcement, rather than give his own ideas about the dioramas, which he thought were stupid anyway. John hated crafty things and was more than happy to let the others take the lead. John's leadership coach always said good managers encourage discussion without pushing an agenda.

"Do you guys remember Mrs. Eisman, the art teacher? When a kid made something really creative, she used to put it up on the wall," Meredith said. "When I was a freshman, I drew a picture of my mom's mixing bowl with a spoon sticking out of it, and Mrs. Eisman loved it. That was the only time I ever had art up on that wall in four years."

One of the other organizers might have said, "Mrs. Eisman never put up my art either." Or even, "Ha ha, nowadays, every kid gets their art put up on the wall, no matter how crappy it is." But Gretchen and Laurie and John said nothing. However, they did silently and simultaneously decide that Meredith would remain outside the reunion planning process.

> 21. Reunion organizers refuse to be associated with losers.

The reunion ended up being a modest success. The Shillelagh Room appeared crowded, but not too crowded, and no one had to wait for a drink. The dioramas were fun—everyone laughed at the one depicting the football players in their feetie pajamas. Laurie got the credit she deserved for being the artistic one of the group. Meredith was able to contact the nametag company, but it was ultimately Gretchen who had to pick up and assemble the nametags, as Meredith's car broke down. Meredith called Gretchen in a panic and even said, "I can take the bus, no problem," but Gretchen told her not to worry about it. John flew in from Europe alone. By that time, he and Matthias had decided to take some time off from their relationship. It was easier anyway, John decided, rather than coming out to everyone from high school.

> 22. Reunion organizers count on winning the award for the person who came the farthest distance to attend the reunion.

Gretchen had too much to drink, something she rarely did. But she was in a celebratory mood, even doing shots of tequila. At one point, she found herself standing next to Meredith, who had come alone. She was wearing makeup and what was probably a new outfit. Her hair was curled softly, and Gretchen did a double take, barely recognizing her. Gretchen thought to say she looked pretty, but because she was drunk by this time, instead she blurted out a question.

"Why did you want to help with the reunion?" Gretchen said. "I mean, we appreciate your help, but why would you even want to come? High school didn't seem like the best time for you."

Meredith didn't seem upset or taken aback. She said, "Yeah, high school wasn't a good time because of most of the people in this room. I guess I wanted to see for myself that everybody has problems, including you, Gretchen. You don't have the perfect life, even though you want everyone to think you do. We're all just trying to make our way in the world." Gretchen felt her face turn red, and struggled to come up with something to say, but then Laurie came by with Petra Mullaly and Lissa Powers, and she didn't even notice that Meredith had walked away.

. . .

Meredith also had a vivid memory of the Challenger explosion. She had been in History class, her assigned seat next to Fred Freitag. She squinted up at the television, deliberately avoiding eye contact with him. It didn't matter—per usual, a stream of obscenities were coming out of his mouth in a monotone, under his breath so that Mr. Romanek wouldn't hear. "Meredith, you're a fugly bitch. I wouldn't even let you suck my dick, although you'd probably look a lot better with my cum all over your face." Then suddenly there were gasps and Mr. Romanek turned up the volume, and the Challenger exploded on TV in front of them. There were huge white contrails streaming out from where the Challenger had been a moment before, and everyone watched silently, not exactly sure what was happening. But after a minute, it was obvious that the Challenger was gone.

Fred Freitag started laughing. Some people were crying. But Meredith was furious. Why couldn't it have been her life ending in a stupendous, fiery televised accident? Sure, it would've been tough on her family initially, but they would heal in time, especially with all the media attention. But no, she was still there, in Mr. Romanek's American History 163 class. She was still in high school, fending off insults from jocks, burnouts, cheerleaders, and even the other dorks. She had to endure Titans of all stripes smacking her on the back of her head as she walked down the hall. She was forced to sit in the front seat of the bus so that the bus driver could police the other Titans who tried to throw gum in her hair. As far as she could tell, there was no end in sight. As the Challenger fell to earth, all Meredith could feel was the relief she might experience in the last moments of her own life.

> 23. Meredith left the reunion around nine-thirty. She had to open at Starbucks the next day.

. . .

Gretchen and Laurie retrieved the dioramas from the Shillelagh Room the following afternoon. Gretchen had an awful headache.

"I don't remember what I said to anyone," she said. "Or what they said to me."

Laurie laughed. "It was a blur, just like high school."

FRANK, WHERE IT'S NICE AND WARM

Caroljean Gavin

FRANK, WHERE IT'S NICE AND WARM

Caroljean Gavin

Frank's mom doesn't want to be a bother. Every Sunday, when I come over to clean her house and cook her week's worth of chicken, meatloaf, spaghetti, and vegetable soup, she follows me around telling me she doesn't want to be a bother.

After I've stripped her bed of the sheets and bedclothes, washed them, and prepared to spread them back out, clean, and refreshed, she sits down on the naked bed as I whip the fitted sheet, opening it up. "I just—" she says, "Really Frank worries too much. I'm fine on my own. You think he'd put me in a home if you didn't show up." More than once I've ballooned the sheet over her head like a child in kindergarten under a parachute. Whenever it happens, she flattens herself down on the bed, shrieks and writhes, and I have to rescue her and fix her a tea and a plate of the butter cookies she likes from the bakery section of the supermarket.

Frank's mom's name is Ruth, short for Ruth-Anne, which was short for Ruth Anne Lowery, which was short for Ruth-Anne Lowery Court. Frank's mom brushes my hair as I'm bending down to put some meat in the oven, "After Frank's dad died, I wasn't sure what I could call myself anymore." She leaves the brush in my hair and deflates down onto a kitchen chair, "How could I still be Mrs. Richard Court? What was I married to a dead man? A ghost? A memory? Maybe he was just a dream. Maybe all those years were just one long dream?"

Frank's mom thinks I should have something more romantic to do with my Sundays. "I know you're not churchy," she says picking socks out of the laundry basket and trying them on her hands like mittens, "Isn't that how you put it? Churchy?" Frank's mom just layers the socks on her hand, not playing with them, simply compiling them, and turning her hand in the daylight, wondering. "But Frank is off Sundays too. He should be taking you somewhere. He should be sweeping you off your feet. He should be marrying you, is what. In a garden. Doesn't have to be churchy. You don't even need a priest. Anyone can marry anyone these days."

She follows me into her bedroom, rummages in the back of a drawer, pulls out a lacy magenta thong and hands it to me. "My gift," Frank's mom says, and I don't have the heart to tell her that I broke up with Frank two years ago because he kept proposing and I kept saying no, and I could see that he'd never understand; I could see that each "no" weighed, that even though he said he loved me no matter what, there were stress fractures. I keep not having the heart to tell her.

I keep not having the heart to tell her why I'm really here.

I never really liked Frank's mom. I never really liked my own mom, or anyone else's mom for that matter. Moms are that tissue paper that's stuffed in shoes still in the shoe store. I mean, they're all crumpled up and shoved where you least expect them, and they take up space in your life in uncomfortable ways. I'm just saying, just speaking from my own experience.

I guess I barely have the heart to tell myself why I'm really here. Frank's mom doesn't have anyone else to take care of her. Frank doesn't like his mother either. But I have also looked deep into Frank's heart, and I have looked deep into Frank's brain, and I have looked deep into Frank's lungs, and I have looked deep into Frank's veins, and to the cute little alcoves of his subconscious, and I know that if Frank's mom dies alone in her apartment eaten by cats, he'll never forgive himself. Also Frank is missing something, and I've been trying to find it in the house. Find it and give it back to him so he can be complete so I don't have to worry about him.

Frank's mom coughs and coughs. Frank's mom stands under the ceiling fan while I dust it to prove to me its not dirty and that even if it was dusty that it wouldn't bother her in the least. "This is killing me," she says, "It's always winter. When are you going to leave me alone?"

After I am done dusting Frank's mom's ceiling fan, I dust Frank's mom, her extra-white permed out hair, her peach sweater, the crease in her slacks I iron into them every week. Her house slippers. Then I tell Frank's mom that I'll see her next week, that if anything comes up she can call me, but if it's an emergency she should call nine-one-one. Frank's mom thanks me, gives me a cold kiss on the cheek, and tells me never to come back again next week.

When I am done cleaning Frank's mom's house and making food for Frank's mom, I go and visit Frank so he can hear that his mom is still his mom, no she hasn't changed, not even for the worse. Frank pours the scotch we used to drink when we were together the nights we made the best love, maybe its nostalgia or maybe its a prayer, I'm not sure. Frank orders dim sum. We take little sips and we take little bites sitting on the little rug in front of his little window spying on his neighbors across the street. Frank's neighbors are polyamorous, and we both wish we had been into that when we were younger. Or maybe just I do. We watch the youngsters hanging off of each other on the porch, bumping music from tiny pill shaped speakers. Well, they're small for speakers, but ginormous for pills. If you took a pill that size, you'd never be sick again—you'd be dead. Clearly, I've been spending too much time with Frank's mom.

Frank's kitchen is spotless, not because he's a neat freak, but because he doesn't use it. I put a leftover dumpling in an empty fridge.

"How are you still alive?" I ask him, sitting back down on his ancient rug, "Do you eat?"

"Well, the takeout always tastes better when you're here," he says, "tastes like home-cooked." There's Frank always coming up with a new line every week, a new way to almost but not quite invite me back. And there's Frank, same as every week, smiling sheepishly, forgetting what he just said, then blushing with embarrassment when he remembers, then slumping down to his side, falling into a snooze, because I drugged his drink when his head was turned.

I heave Frank over just a little, just so I can pull his sweater up past his shoulder blades, take out the little screwdriver and open up the hatch in his back. I didn't put the thing there. I just didn't ask any questions when I discovered it. At first I thought it was a horrific scar. I tried not to look at it, and then one night, one night after he passed out after sex, I got a little bored, a little curious.

Once I have Frank open, I just shove his mom's magenta panties in there. Look, it's not my first choice, but it's all I have, and maybe it'll get him in touch with his feminine side, or make him feel sexy to other women, or just give him really weird-ass dreams about his mom.

Week after that, Frank's mom nearly drowns in the toilet because she tried to use it after I cleaned it leaving the seat up, so I tie a ribbon from my wrist to hers so she doesn't get lost. This does not dampen her spirits. It is a long ribbon. She is constantly whipping it up into ripples like it's a jump rope. She is transfixed. When I find a box of jingle bells under her bed she begs me to sew some to her socks. "I always wanted to be musical," she says, "But I kept forgetting that I was obsessed with learning the violin." I obey her wishes and pocket an extra bell for later.

"You bug your mom like this?" she asks me, wiggling her ankle while I'm trying to gently push the needle through her thick white socks without stabbing her skin.

I do not see my mom. My mom does not see me; she split a long, long, long, long time ago, day before elementary school graduation. Dad was too distraught to come. Dad was too distraught to clean the house that summer, to feed himself, to do anything but marinate in his room surrounded by the relics of his marriage, stewing in the juices of incomprehensibility. "You harass Frank like this when he comes over?"

It's ok to say that because we are joking, because she is harsh and insensitive and expects me to be as well, but she just leans all the way over and starts crying onto her newly attached bells. I wipe her tears with a tissue and then pocket it.

She sneaks a hand to my belly. "You and Frank should have kids, right now," she says, "You should have them now. They won't love you right, but maybe Frank would come over if he had kids to show off."

"Could you even hold a baby without breaking it," I deflect.

"Ha!" she coughs, "Probably not, probably break its head, and oof, I mean look at that nose of yours, poor kid wouldn't be starting right as it was."

Frank has a noticeable hip swish now, with a little wiggle, like he's trying to work something out of his ass crack. I follow him to our usual rug picnic, with a bag of samosas, chana masala, and roasted lamb, along with some strong brewed black iced tea, a special one for him and one for me.

"I've missed you," he says, leaning over, stroking my hand with his. "You're skin feels so good."

"Ugh," I say. His touch was way too light and now I'm itchy. "I think your mom is losing it," I say.

"Ugh," he echoes. "Do you really come all this way to talk about my mom?"

I take a huge chunk of lamb. Its succinct, juicy, luscious, flavors wash over my tongue, and I almost goddamned cry.

"We're friends, right?" he asks, washing the sting of a samosa out with a huge swig of tea.

"Of course," I say, "And as your friend, I think, Frank, your mom needs—"

"What kind of friends though?" he asks.

My mouth is on fire. I am stupid to where this is going.

"Friends that—?" he asks.

I shake my head, but when he lunges at me tongue first, I cannot resist. The truth is I love Frank. The truth is I fucking love Frank. The truth is that every time I leave Frank I go home and go crazy with the vibrator, and its Frank, and I smell him and feel him, like I am smelling him and feeling him now, stripping him down, being stripped down by him, and mounting him with the curtains open, oh man, let those kids across the street see how the adults do it.

By some miracle we crest together, and as I fall over Frank's chest, he falls into his usual "slumber." Thank God we never were the missionary types. He would have crushed me.

I nudge him over.

Trace the lines of the hatch in his back. Trace the lines like a scar. Like something hurt him once upon a time. I wish I could heal it. I wish I could heal Frank's need for me. I think I am making it worse. I lay my head on his sweaty back. I could just leave now, once and for all, and forever. I cover his back in tears.

The screwdriver is in my pants across the room.

So far.

I grab it. And the bell, and the tissues.

It's for the best.

Dad was so distraught when mom left. Dad was so distraught, so disappointed he forgot there were other things to love about life. He forgot there was me.

The following Sunday, I shuffle into Frank's mom's

house, paper grocery bags digging into my hips.

Frank's mom is sitting on the couch. Knitting something. Something that might be a baby blanket.

"Hey Ruth," I call on my way to her kitchen.

"Hey yourself," she calls back, but she does not get up. She does not follow me. She does not shadow me with an impromptu soft shoe. She does not sneak up and try to give me a wet willy. She does not get stuck in the couch. She just sits there like a person.

The kitchen is spotless. Even the microwave, and the fridge is full of a week's worth of prepared meals. Freaked out that she's been starving herself, forgetting to eat, I look, and it's stuff I didn't make, stuff I don't know how to make.

There are no clothes in her hamper. They are clean in her drawers or ironed and hung in the closet.

No stains in the toilet bowl, no toothpaste splatters on the mirror.

I stomp out to her, "Old woman," I call.

She holds up her knitting. "Do you want a girl or a boy?" she asks, "I made it green. Good for either. Bad for both."

"What's going on?" I ask, "You seeing another housekeeper behind my back?"

She pats the cushion next to her. "Sit your ass down." She purses her lips.

I sit like a child.

"I told you I didn't need you," she says. "Not your pity. Not Frank's. I can take care of myself."

"You can't," I say. "You can barely walk around your own apartment without getting tangled in the curtains."

"Oh that?" She sweeps out a knitting needle. "That stuff's just for fun."

"You've been fucking with me this whole time?"

"Mad you're not the only one, lady?" She wraps up her knitting, pushes it all into a bag and then onto my lap. "You figure out how to finish it. You can use it for your bed. At your place. So you don't freeze at night while sleeping alone."

I take the bag and fidget with it, staring at my stupid fidgeting fingers. The bleeding coral nail polish I tried is chipping like hell. "I'm not going to say I'm sorry," I said, "I still care, you know. I can't leave, leave."

Frank's mom kicks off her slippers, one soars all the way to the TV hitting the dark screen. "You imagine leaving means you don't care. Sometimes you leave because you care. Maybe it's because you don't want to be left. Huh? You think Frank doesn't talk to me? You imagine Frank never calls?" She pokes me in the side with the remote control.

"I thought you liked me coming here?" I say, pouting.

"Girl, I like you. You're a pain in the ass, so of course I love you. But I am not your mom. You as crazy and willful, fun and infuriating as you are. You are not my daughter. Not in any way."

I stand up. Left in place. "That's it then?" I ask, "You at least want me to take out your trash?"

"Nah," she says, "That cute Greek widower from across the street did it for me last night."

"Did what for you?" I swing the knitting bag at her, batting it against her pantyhosed knee.

"Hey, there's a box of Frank's old papers by the door. Take it to him."

I grab it, and walk out of the house without saying goodbye, without waving, without even flipping her off.

Frank's big box o'shit is just a regular carton-type box

with a lid. I sit it in my passenger's seat. Should I string the seat belt across it? It's not a person. It's not Frank. But it might be. Inside, it's just papers, loose papers, notebooks, journals, letters, greeting cards, most that were sent to him, a few that he wrote but never sent. They look to be stories, poems, letters, etcetera from when Frank was a little boy up until, I guess, up until he graduated college and finally moved out of his mother's house.

My Dog
By Frank Court
Age 7 and ½

My dog is name is
Cinnamon and she is
Brown and red and pretty neat
Her whole body smells
Like the bottom of her feet

Another:

Frankie,

Dude can you believe that bitch Mrs. Cox? Mrs. Cocks! Ha! She's a bitch. I'm in detention because she said I was cheating. She wouldn't know cheating if it bit her flappy ass. Anyway are you coming to the show on Saturday? We have an extra ticket. It's thirty dollars.

Vinny

There seemed to be no rhyme or reason to what Frank kept. But Frank was kind of a pack rat. He never really wanted to get rid of anything.

Dear Mallory,

It's been one hundred forty seven days, twelve hours and fourteen minutes since I kissed you goodbye, but every time I close my eyes all I can see is your face, your beautiful eyes, your smiling cheeks, your adorable dimples. I hope you're doing well in all of your classes, so you can graduate fast and come home to me. You are the love of my life. I miss you so much. You will always be the love of my life. Please write back soon.

I ransack the box for a picture of this Mallory, but there isn't one, just a handful of letters he wrote and apparently never sent to her. I stuff them in my pocket and pull out of Frank's mom's driveway.

When I get to Frank's house, I can hear music, pushing against the front door. I ring the bell and I knock, but he doesn't answer. I try the knob, and it is locked, so I pull out the key I still have and let myself in to find Frank on the couch bent over a guitar I have never seen in my life, playing it like he can play the guitar and singing, not words, but sounds, vowels, just joining the music of strings and fingers with music of voice.

I sit down next to him, my pockets full of old love letters he never sent to some other girl. I didn't stop for food. We can order something if he's hungry, but I'm just sitting there, sitting there next to him, watching the effects of the bell and his mother's tears and wondering if I ever really knew Frank at all.

After about twenty minutes, Frank opens his eyes like from a dream and almost jumps out of his skin when he sees me. The guitar slips from his grip and thunks to the floor.

"Shit," he says, "How long have you been here?"

"Forever," I say staring at him, pissed at my own presence for breaking his spell.

"No, really?" he asks.

"A little while. I like your song."

"I don't know, it's just something I came up with. Feels more like the guitar is playing me than the other way around. You know what I mean?"

"No." No I don't.

"Well anyway—" he picks up the guitar and latches it in a case. "How are you? How's mom?"

"I guess I could ask you that," I say. "Have you been in on this the whole time?"

"On what now?" he asks, with no clue on his face or voice.

"She knew we aren't together."

"Sorry," Frank says, "I didn't know it was a secret. I actually didn't know you didn't tell her. I told her about this woman at work I had a thing for, and she nearly lost her mind."

"Oh. You're dating. I didn't know you were dating."

"Aren't you? Aren't you dating?"

I shake my head. Well, I guess I did it right? Hooray! Made Frank whole. He didn't need me anymore. "Who would I date?" I ask him. "It was over for me when I met you."

"Oh," he says, "Just oh."

And I don't know what I'm doing, but I don't have time to drug him, so I just order him to take off his shirt, and he smiles while he does it, and I turn him around, and I take out my little screwdriver, while he's standing there completely awake, and I open his hatch, and he laughs and asks what I'm doing, and I ask him how can he date someone else when he doesn't even know himself, and I open that hatch, and nothing falls out, not the bell, tissue, panties any of it, they have grown into him. "How do you feel?" I ask him, and he laughs.

I plunge my hand into his back, reach around for his heart, hold it in my hands. "How do you feel now?" I ask.

He cries. "You left," he says. "You should leave if you're going to leave, you know, you should."

And I know I should, I fucking know it.

It's warm inside Frank. His heart tingles my palm. Something about his blood and muscles playing over my skin makes my brain hum. If I could step inside Frank, I would live inside Frank, curled up against his spine, be carried everywhere with him, grow into his tissues, but his hatch isn't big enough. It's not big enough, yet I push my arms in, push in my head; I know I can't stay like this, just legs trailing behind his legs. "How do you feel now?"

"The same," he says, "The same, you fucking idiot, don't you know how a part of me you are?"

Frank stretches to let me in. I smell myself in there with him, my shampoo, my laughter in the wind with the turkey legs and dirt of renaissance festivals, and I smell his mom in there too, baking cinnamon rolls for his birthday, sitting out in the rain watching his baseball games, pushing lavender into his sock drawer, creating love one hopeless moment at a time, never leaving, not even when restless, not even when afraid.

IMAGINARY CREATURES

Charles Conley

IMAGINARY CREATURES

Charles Conley

1. Molly: Tuesday Morning

"Everyone here is so proud of you, sweetheart," the lady said to Molly. "Just a few more questions, and we'll be done." The lady smiled at Molly's mom when she said this, but it wasn't a real smile. "Can you tell me what you were doing last night before it came?"

"Sleeping?"

"You were asleep?"

No she wasn't sleeping. She was pouting and squeezing Ernest, her moose, and listening to the sounds from the TV downstairs. Zach was watching his shows. She couldn't hear the words they were saying, but she could hear the car crashes and blow-ups. She didn't know why Zach watched scary shows.

"Oh, no. I was . . . Ernest was on the ground," Molly said. She must have fallen asleep for a second, because then the TV wasn't on anymore, and Ernest was gone. Her mom and dad—not her dad, her stepdad—were talking in their room on the other side of the stairway, and just like with the TV, she couldn't hear the words, only the blow-ups. Molly looked at the lady and tried not to cry. "And I couldn't get him, because I heard the monster.

And if it heard me move, it would know I wasn't asleep."

"I understand, sweetheart." The lady patted Molly's knee. "So the monster doesn't come if you pretend you're asleep?"

"Not if I'm quiet and don't move."

"Does anything else keep the monster away?"

She didn't like to think so hard about the monster, but it was okay here because there were so many people, her mom, and the lady and her partner. The partner looked mean, but maybe that meant he wouldn't be afraid. Molly looked up at the ceiling to think, and her bangs fell in her eyes. Her mom brushed them out for her, and then she started to nod but stopped herself. Why wouldn't she help? Molly wanted to whisper the answers to her mom and have her mom tell the lady what Molly said, but her mom wouldn't let her. She never helped anymore. The lady wasn't mean like her partner, but Molly felt shy.

"If the blanket's up all the way over my head."

"Okay," the lady wrote it down. "Anything else?"

If the nightlight is on the monster won't come either, but her mom didn't turn on the nightlight last night. When Molly reminds her, and says she's afraid of the monster, her mom says it's just her imagination, and even though Molly knows her mom's wrong, she feels like she's making her mom sad. So she didn't ask last night, about the nightlight, and then the monster came. But Molly could tell her mom was already sad now, and she didn't want to make her feel sadder, so she said, "I don't think so."

Before she and her mom moved here, she could sleep in her mom's bed when she was scared, and when she was with her dad, he would come in her room and lie down with her until she felt better. But here it wasn't like that.

"Okay. We're going to try to draw a picture of what it looks like," the lady said. "Let's start with how it moves."

"Slow," Molly said. "Quiet."

Molly's stepdad came from the kitchen carrying a tray with a coffee pot and milk and sugar. In case anybody wanted more. He held the tray in front of the lady's partner, who stood next to the wall. Her stepdad talked to the man while the man fixed his coffee. Molly couldn't hear what they were talking about because the lady was asking her a question.

"Do you think, does it have legs?"

"Yeah," Molly said. "Wait."

"Of course, sweetheart."

The lady took a loud sip of coffee. If Molly had done that her mom would say, "No slurping." The lady put her mug down on the coffee table and rearranged the pad of yellow paper on her lap and fixed her skirt. Her mom's leg was touching Molly's all the time because her mom didn't trust the lady.

"It has three legs, I'm pretty sure," Molly said. "They're short and fat." The lady didn't nod or say anything, so Molly kept talking. "The feet are really big and soft. That's why it's so quiet. They squish down when it walks so you don't hear the steps, just creaking."

"You're so good at this. Does it have arms too?"

"Unh-uh."

"Are you sure?"

"Uh-huh."

The lady flipped through her notes. "You said it moved the boxes, that you could hear them sliding out of the way. Do you know how it moves them?"

"Oh." Molly looked up at the ceiling again. "It uses

its nose."

"Ah. Of course. How long is its neck? What does the face look like?"

Molly had never seen the monster, but she could picture it like she could picture Ernest even though he was upstairs on her bed. So Molly thought hard and described the monster, with a neck longer than a dog's but shorter than a giraffe's, with its squishy face and body, with its big nose the size of a teddy bear and its even bigger mouth. Her stepdad was still over by the man, but now they were listening to her answers and not talking. Her stepdad still had little black and white whiskers on his face and his hair was sticking up and he was wearing just jeans and a t-shirt, and the other man had on a suit and his hair was brushed and his face was shaved. Molly could tell this bothered her stepdad and she felt bad for him.

Molly was wondering how to describe the monster's eyes and mouth when Zach came in the room. He had his black jeans and a t-shirt on for school and was wearing his backpack. The adults looked at him like when Molly's carrying the tea set and they think she's going to drop it. Especially his dad.

She answered the woman's questions, but really wanted Zach to come over and sit with her. He would help, not like her mom. And he knew about the monster.

In the wall past the foot of her bed were two short wooden doors with slats in them. Behind them was the crawlspace, where the monster lived. It could hear everything she did through the slats. The doors had small white doorknobs, and the magnet on the left door didn't work anymore, so a purple scrunchie looped around the doorknobs to keep them shut. But the scrunchie wasn't strong enough to stop the monster.

The crawlspace was low and narrow and went from her room to her mom's room along the front of the house. The wooden floor gave her splinters, and she wasn't allowed to touch the insulation, which looked like cotton candy. She'd peeked inside lots of times but didn't go all the way in until Zach took her one time. He had a flashlight and they went down the tunnel, past her mom's dresses to where the boxes with the Christmas ornaments were. He showed her the square panel that opened up behind her mom's bed. Zach said when he was her age, a monster used to live back there. Then he realized what he said and showed her with the flashlight how it wasn't there anymore.

But now Molly knew what all those angry noises she heard at night were. The monster must have been hiding because it was daytime or because of the flashlight, or maybe it was afraid of Zach. She didn't know why, but she knew it still lived there when no one was looking, and that one night it would come get her in her room.

Zach sat on the chair opposite the lady and winked at Molly, and then she felt better. Zach listened to what Molly was saying. Molly looked at him while she described the monster, because he knew what it looked like, to make sure she was doing it right, and she must have been, because Zach didn't say anything until Molly described the monster's teeth. Then he said in a voice like he didn't want to bother anyone, "I think the teeth are different than that. I think they're not sharp, but like a whole mouth full of molars."

"What's molars?" Molly asked him. The partners looked at each other.

"Back teeth," Zach said. "The ones you use on crunchy things. Like bones." He scrunched up his nose.

"Oh yeah," Molly said. "That's right."

"You're sure?" the lady said.

"Uh-huh," Molly said, looking at Zach.

The lady didn't say anything for a little bit and then said, "That makes sense."

2. Zach: Tuesday Evening

Zach was trying to watch TV. Since his mom died, it was harder to find stuff to talk about at school. With the guys. With anyone. And TV shows were something—pretty much the only thing—he could have a conversation about without people looking like they just wanted him to go away. Or him feeling like he was going to cry. But he was distracted. He couldn't get comfortable on the couch with these pillows. The armrest was wood with only a thin layer of fabric over it, and it was too hard without a pillow, but the new pillows had too much stuffing. His neck cramped when he used them. That was when he was lying down with his legs on the couch. The other position had him slouching on the couch, facing the TV directly with his feet up on the coffee table. But the rules about feet on the coffee table had never been clarified. Sometimes Janet would say, "People eat off of that table, you know," or just say his name in exasperation, and other times she wouldn't say anything at all. When there were guests, she was more likely to say something, and those people were in the kitchen, talking with his dad and Janet while they all waited for the thing in the crawlspace to show up. Really it wasn't the pillows, it was their talking that kept him from paying attention to the show.

He couldn't hear all or even most of the conversation, just some words. He could hear the tone, though, and that was what had his attention. For once in his life, adults weren't acting as if they always knew everything. After straining to hear for a while, he went into the kitchen to see for himself. He chugged half a glass of iced tea so he could pretend he was in there to get a refill and not to listen in on their conversation. Adults don't want you to listen when they're like that.

The four of them were sitting around the kitchen table drinking coffee. Same as the couch pillows, Janet brought in the kitchen table after she and his dad got married. It wasn't like Janet and Molly had brought that much furniture when they moved in, but what they did bring felt like it changed everything around. Zach had no specific objection to the kitchen table, just that it was different. His mom never ate at this one. The man sat with a laptop in front of him, which had a wire connecting it to a PA on the counter. White noise came from the PA, and the man was talking over it.

"Real, imaginary; imaginary, real," he said. "We don't determine that. We record the creature in as much detail as we can. That's our job."

"But then what *happens*?" his father said. "Come on. We can't be the first people who want to know."

"Of course not," the man said. "But we have to be as accurate as possible here."

Janet fetched the coffee pot and refilled everyone's mugs, which was the kind of thing she'd do when what she really wanted to do was yell at you. "So what's the difference between real and imaginary?" she asked while she poured. "If there's no difference, why use different words?"

Zach stood at the refrigerator, ignored by the adults and forgetting to pretend he was doing something else.

Janet sat back down next to his father and moved her chair away from him a little.

The woman answered this time. "Honestly, the Society has a whole department of philosophers and scientists working on that question."

"That's your answer? How old is your organization and you still haven't bothered to come up with an answer?"

"Well, the American Chimerical Society has existed for just over forty years, but its precursor was around for a couple of centuries before that, and people have been doing this work in a more or less organized fashion for—what?—about a millennium and half?" the man said. "So how long depends on when you start counting."

"And it's not that we don't have an answer—there's always an answer," the woman partner took over again. There was a wheeze from the PA. Janet and Zach's dad stared at it, and the two partners closed their eyes and listened. Molly must have mumbled in her sleep or something, because there were no other sounds. After a long minute, the woman continued speaking. "It's just that it keeps changing: we learn more, philosophical and theological systems change, certain ideas come into or go out of fashion. There's a paper updated biannually with our official position—I can get you the current version."

"Could you summarize it for us?" Janet said.

"I'm afraid not," the woman said. "It's far too complicated."

"Well that's a big help," Zach's father said.

"I know," the woman said. "Sorry." Her partner took a deep breath as if he was going to start talking, but the woman continued. "Look, practically speaking, here's what I think: The difference between a real creature and an imaginary creature is simply this: once we record it—assuming we get it down accurately—if it's still around, it's real."

His dad and Janet waited for her to finish her thought, but she didn't. When they realized she wasn't going to continue, they looked surprised, as if the super-complicated answer they'd been expecting was actually really simple. Then they both made faces that showed they didn't know what she was talking about. Almost any other time, Zach would have cracked up at their sequence of expressions.

"So if it turns out to be imaginary, that means it was always imaginary." Janet said.

"That gets into semantics," the man cut in before his partner. "Also, it's not our department. We've already said more than we're supposed to." He scowled. "Our assignment is to come onsite and record the creature as comprehensibly as possible, first via interviews, then whenever possible by direct observation."

Zach couldn't listen anymore and went back to the living room. The man was talking bureaucratic bullshit, and the woman was telling half the truth.

His mom had tried to warn him. At the end. No one told Zach it was the end, but he figured it out even before his mom was in a hospital bed in the den and not sleeping upstairs anymore. She'd climbed the stairs every night for as long as she could. Zach heard her from his room. Once he noticed how long it took her to get up the stairs, he started noticing everything else: like how much Chinese food and pizza they were eating; like how much more TV she watched, but how little she cared about what was on; like how she wore the same black sweatpants and thick red sweater with the roll neck every day and how her breath started to smell bad, similar to a piece of meat you floss out from between your teeth when your gums swell up. It's not like they hadn't told him she was sick, just not how sick. When they set up the bed in the den and a nurse started coming—first once a day, then a few times a day, and then all the time—he knew it was serious. When his dad started sleeping on the couch downstairs at night, Zach knew it was hopeless.

Zach would come home from school and the nurse would take a break to do whatever—take a walk outside, or eat, or talk on the phone. Zach would sit on the edge of his mom's bed, and she would talk as much as she could, until she was too weak or her throat hurt too much. Like she was trying to cram in everything she would have told him the rest of his life.

When she couldn't talk, she would point at the CD-player, and Zach would put on an album, Joan Baez or Joni Mitchell or Judy Collins, some folksinger, usually a woman. Before his mom was ill she was always singing along in her pretty but too-high voice, even when she was driving him and his friends around in the car. His friends would make fun of her, after, impersonating her, but like she was singing opera instead of how she was really singing, which was sweet and clear and not at all how they did it. He wanted to punch his friends in the face, remembering how they'd made fun of her. But no one did anymore. They didn't talk about her at all.

The show Zach was trying to watch was a remake of some cheesy seventies show, which for some reason the guys at school liked. Zach couldn't imagine even in the seventies it could be any worse than this. A woman almost died in some accident and they replaced some parts of her with robot parts that made her stronger and faster.

Did people used to believe that you could lose a part of yourself and get it replaced and have it be even better than before? No one believed that now. When you lose something, you lose it forever, and that was what getting old was—losing one thing after another until everything was gone. The episode was almost over, and it ended exactly the same way every episode ended, and the whole thing was a predictable waste of time—which didn't mean the guys wouldn't be talking about it tomorrow. Especially about how hot the girl was, which Zach didn't even agree with anyway. As soon as the commercials came on, he was back in the den with his mother.

On days when it was really bad, when she could hardly talk at all, Zach would sit and drink chocolate milk and listen to music with her, watch her lie there and breathe, cry when she was too conked out on all the drugs to notice. But she talked when she could. One of the last times they had a real conversation before she stopped making sense, she'd told Zach about what he was like when he was a baby. Later she would talk to Zach as if he was his dad, and she'd talk about the baby, who was Zach, or she'd talk to Zach as if he was still a baby. But she wasn't doing that yet—she knew who she was talking to and how old Zach really was. She'd said when she looked at him, she could still see him as a baby. He'd turned out just like she used to imagine he would. She knew he'd be smart, because even watching him play in the crib you could tell there was a whole world going on behind his eyes. She didn't mean IQ smart. He'd do fine in school, she didn't worry about that, but she wasn't talking about books. He was creative. He had imagination. But he had to be careful, because sometimes the world didn't like that.

Zach was too stupid to understand. He could picture her face while she was saying it, and now he could see how frustrated she'd been—between how sick she was and how much harder it was becoming for her to concentrate and how you can't talk about some things with the people you really love. But everything she'd said at the end she'd said with that same intensity, and how was Zach supposed to know that this one thing was the most important one? Everything she said felt like the most important thing.

The theme music for the next show came on, and it wasn't one he watched. Hardly anyone at school did either, so he didn't bother paying attention. He was thinking about his mom and what she'd said and how he couldn't make the same mistake again.

A couple of weeks after his mom died, he started going to a shrink. It wasn't like he was forced to go, but his dad wanted him to, and he was trying to make things easier on his dad. He didn't think it could hurt, so he went.

The shrink told him his father worried about him. It didn't matter that Zach was doing everything he could to make his dad not worry. The shrink said his father heard Zach talking to himself at night and crying, sometimes really loud. Like crying was some kind of crime. And Zach had acted just like Molly this afternoon, like a kid who doesn't know better, sitting on a couch answering an adult's questions the best he could while the adult wrote the answers down.

Zach explained he wasn't talking to himself, he was talking to his mother. He said he pictured his mom sitting on the edge of his bed, in the soft white dressing gown and thick blue and white striped robe she used to wear on special days, like Mother's Day or Christmas, mornings when she didn't have to shower and get dressed first thing. On those days, his dad would bumble around the kitchen to give his mom a morning off. His scrambled eggs were good, and he didn't burn the toast, but it took him a long time, and Zach and his mom could just whatever. Hang out. That's what she wore now at night, and it was like she'd been in her own room sleeping and had just come in to talk to him. So they would talk. And they'd cry. And it was so sad because he thought when she went away this time, she'd really be gone, and there's no way you can say everything to someone, even when you know it's the last time. Even when they're not real. He never saw her leave, he just eventually fell asleep, and when he woke up later—not in the morning, he wasn't sleeping through the night yet—he felt so bad, like he was weak and stupid and worthless. Falling asleep on her was the worst betrayal he could think of. His dad wasn't enforcing bedtime those days, so Zach would stay up as late as he could watching TV or playing video games. He dreaded going to bed and having all those feelings that he knew he would have. Not every night, but most nights.

The shrink looked up from his notebook and said everything Zach described was normal. It's not like Zach was delusional—he knew his mother wasn't really there. It was part of the healing process. But maybe instead of keeping it to himself like that, Zach should maybe try to talk to his dad, to his friends, or to the shrink, instead.

Then his mom stopped coming. Or, not on her own. He could, what, like force it. Concentrate and almost convince himself she was there. But the words she was supposed to be saying would be in his voice, not hers. He didn't really feel her there, he only pretended to. He tried three or four times, but it was always that way, and he gave up. That's when he understood what his mom had tried to tell him, about protecting his imagination, and it was too late to do any good. At least for her.

As stupid as he'd been, he didn't stay stupid. Whenever the shrink wanted to get all emotional vampire on him after that, make Zach live through all the pain again, Zach would tell him stories, give the shrink just what he wanted, but he never told him the truth again. He'd tell the shrink these sad stories—even cry—but it was all fake. And it felt good. Not only was Zach protecting what he really thought and felt and imagined, but he was using the lies to get revenge against the only person he could find to blame anything on. Sometimes that was the worst part—that his mom died, and it wasn't anybody's fault, not even his dad's, not really even the doctor's. If he could just find someone to hate, to focus all the anger on, then maybe he could stop hating everyone, people who were happy or could pretend they were happy.

When he stopped talking to his mom at night, it was like his dad must have thought all of a sudden Zach was over it, which was fine with Zach. He didn't hate his dad—he felt bad for him, because he lost her too, and because he was an adult, so he had all those stupid adult rules about how he could act—but he couldn't talk to him. What would they do? Sit around and cry and hug each other? Zach just tried to make it so his dad didn't worry about him, which his dad was always ready to do. Which everybody was always ready to do. Except Molly. She was the only one who didn't treat him like a time bomb.

An explosion on TV startled Zach and the glass slipped out of his hands and broke on the ground, spilling iced tea over the carpet. He must have dozed off. He rubbed his eyes, picked up the biggest parts of broken glass and the ice. As he approached the kitchen door, he heard Janet's voice and stopped. She said something like "I just want an answer!" or "how is that an answer?" and it got louder so that by the word "answer" she was almost yelling.

His dad said, "They're just doing their job," which was his response when Zach said they should sue his mom's doctors or key their cars or something. It was his dad's great excuse. As Zach expected, Janet snapped at him.

"Actually, their job is to make this better. In case you haven't noticed, that's not what's happening."

Then his dad did that thing that drove Janet just as crazy as it drove Zach, when he made excuses for you to someone else right in front of your face. He could practically see his dad acting all humble as he said to the partners, "We haven't been getting a lot of sleep..."

Rather than escalating, Janet lowered her voice. "You've never asked yourself these questions?"

Zach opened the door and the creaking of the hinges drowned out the beginning of the man's response. Zach heard him finish, "but asking, and being qualified to answer are two different beasts. So to speak."

They were all in the same positions around the table, and they were still agitated, but in a different, more general way. Where before they were ready to jump out of their seats at the slightest crackle from the PA, now it was like any excuse would do. They weren't being polite and formal anymore, hiding what they really thought about what someone was saying. Everyone was either annoyed at having to keep answering the same stupid questions or angry because they were confused by the answers.

The lady huffed at her partner's answer. "Here's the way I look at it," she said. "And obviously, I'm not providing the *official* answer, which I said I'd get you. In the end, it's about defining the words. What I think is: until we record it, there's just no difference between the real and the imaginary." Zach couldn't believe they were still talking about this.

Janet looked like she wanted to refill their coffee again, but instead she turned to Zach. "What's up honey?"

"I'm sorry. I spilled my drink on the carpet and broke the glass."

The PA was still buzzing in the background, but no one paid attention to it anymore. Everyone had coffee mugs in front of them, and there were scraps of paper on the table that had words with circles around them and lines and arrows drawn between them. A couple of pieces had fallen on the floor.

"Come on, Zach," Janet snapped. She started to stand up.

"No, no. I'll clean it up. Just—just tell me how."

"No, I'll . . ." Janet said. "It'll be quicker if I just do it." She looked pissed, definitely, but also as if cleaning up his mess was better than being stuck in that conversation another second.

3. Janet: Wednesday Evening

Janet came down to the kitchen after putting Molly to bed and found Steve looking over the shoulder of the man from the Society as he set up his computer. It was a laptop, and the man was basically just plugging in the speaker and the power cord, so there was nothing for Steve to do. If he wanted to make himself useful, he should have made the coffee. Janet measured out the coffee grounds and poured in the water. She turned on the coffee maker, set the pastries Steve had picked up on the way home from work out on a plate, and brought the plate to the table. The woman was going through some paperwork and studying the sketch of the monster they'd frightened Molly with right before bed.

The last time Janet wanted a cigarette this badly was after her ex-husband moved out. She'd been off cigarettes over five years by that point, but when she found herself alone, she picked them up as if she'd never stopped. She chain-smoked past the point where it hurt, knocking out half a pack between when she put Molly down and went to bed herself, exhausted but unsleeping. She smoked out on the porch—it was spring—and the occasional car driving by or a plane overhead, the croaking of the frogs starting back up after a quiet winter, all combined with the sounds from the monitor she kept next to her, a few minutes of Molly rustling in bed before slow and steady breathing indicated she'd fallen asleep. When Molly was with her ex, Janet would go through a pack and a half, two packs a day, smoking rather than eating, crying most of the time, sometimes alone and sometimes with friends.

She cried all spring. Strangely, during the winter they tried to save their marriage, she hardly cried at all. She'd been violently angry, she'd been terrified, she'd been sentimental and needy, she'd been unsure about what to do, but she hadn't fallen into that simple abject sadness. As if sadness only came after, once the worst had happened. Everything before that was a struggle with and against hope; sadness only showed up once she understood there was no hope left.

She had no cigarettes here, but on her way to the table she changed course and retrieved a bottle of red wine, an opener, and four glasses. The coffee last night only made the waiting harder; she was tense enough without the caffeine. She opened the bottle, poured herself a glass, and drank without letting the wine breathe. She looked at Steve, daring him to say something, but he just signaled to pour him one as well. The two partners stuck with coffee.

Everyone was in the same seat as the night before—on the other side of the table, the man sat with his computer in the seat near the electrical outlet with the woman next to him. Steve sat on the same side as Janet. Their chairs were too close together. She wanted to move away not because their marriage was falling apart, but because she wanted to be able to see everyone's faces at the same time while they were talking. She didn't move away. The hissing of the monitor, which she noticed in the silence after she sat down, explained the cigarette craving—it was the same noise she would always associate with that long, sad spring.

The coffee machine gurgled. Janet got back up, took out two mugs, the sugar and milk, and poured coffee for the two bestiagraphers. Just like last night, the four of them sat quietly and listened to the monitor, and just like last night, all they heard was Molly tossing and turning a couple of times before she fell asleep. Until Molly settled, the air was charged with possibility, but once she did, the quiet of the room became hollow rather than anticipatory, like the difference between depression and anxiety. Janet was right on the edge of falling once more into that emptiness, and this, combined with her desire for a cigarette, made her want to pick a fight.

The woman, as if she could hear Janet's thoughts and wanted to help, looked at her. "I was thinking about your question last night, about if the creature turns out to be imaginary, whether that means it was always imaginary.

For me, that's the most perplexing question about this whole process. It's what keeps me at it, I think." The man started doing something more vigorous on his computer, something that involved striking the keyboard forcefully, as if to prove he wasn't listening. "But all I can think is . . ." She nodded her head several times. "I fell for this surfer one time, oh my god, so hard. It didn't last long—I was doing my junior year abroad in Australia, and we didn't even meet until March or so—"

Her partner looked up from the monitor. "Funny you say that," he said, forcing a chuckle. "I was just thinking about that case they tell us about during training. You know, the Australian one. It's like a . . . cautionary tale." Janet ignored him and his cautionary tale. She was disgusted with these two and their ridiculous job and their moronic work stories and this endless goddamn waiting. She wished the woman had been allowed to continue speaking. Maybe she could help Janet understand.

She'd met her ex just about ten years ago, when she hadn't been worried about marriage or kids or what kind of love it takes to make a family. She found in him the things she'd been looking for—attraction, excitement, proximity. No one told her that what you should look for in a husband is different. No one warned her that the good-looking, outgoing, passionate man she was falling in love with had more needs than any one woman could satisfy for long, especially when he only knew the one way to satisfy them.

"So obviously, it's got to be imaginary, right?" The man was worked up. "Even if there were multiple reports all confirming the same details—the duck bill, the funny-shaped body? Eggs!" Steve was listening to the man's story; his partner must have heard it a million times. Janet went back to her own thoughts and didn't even pretend she was paying attention.

Janet had just been pissed that her ex had accepted another project! "It's an important project," he'd said on the phone. "I'm sorry baby. I'll be home as soon as I can." There had been times when Janet suspected an affair—when he was late at work or had to go into the office during the weekend—but this wasn't one of them. He was always so convincing—telling her she was imagining things—that she'd stopped suspecting anything. That night had been an especially difficult one with Molly, and Janet got it into her head that Molly wouldn't fall asleep until she said goodnight to her father, even though Molly was too young to even say the word goodnight yet. Janet had used every trick she knew and invented a few new ones in order to get Molly down, and she was exhausted. But she couldn't just go to sleep and waste the righteousness of that anger, without reminding him that he'd promised no new projects for a while, not until Molly was sleeping better, not until things settled down a little. Of course he couldn't turn down a project at work, they both knew that, not with the possibility of a promotion, not when they needed to make up for her foregone salary. She just wanted him to understand how things were for her, make him see how stressful it was. Let him comfort her. He'd always been good at that.

But he didn't even try. He was so quiet coming into the room, into bed, she thought he was being considerate and almost let him go to sleep. Instead she started the speech, the one she'd been rehearsing the whole time she waited. She didn't get far before he broke in. He, it seemed, had his own speech prepared, and she was so stunned by his response—angry defensiveness rather than contrition and comfort—that he had the whole thing out before she spoke again.

Zach slunk into the room and the man stopped talking. Zach was creeping around in the corners as if he was afraid he would be in the way. Was he still upset about last night?

"Zach, honey, I'm sorry I snapped when you spilled your drink."

Zach looked up as if he was surprised at being addressed, or like she'd caught him doing something wrong. "What? Oh, no. I'm sorry. For making a mess."

"I know you are. Don't feel bad. It all came up. There's no stain."

"That's good," he said and left the kitchen without getting whatever he'd come in for.

Her ex, in his speech, talked about the pressure she put on him, the disintegration of their sex life since Molly was born, how uncomfortable he was at home, always on edge, always waiting to be criticized. He wondered whatever happened to the fun they used to have together, the late nights drinking, talking, sharing everything, also, again, the sex. He complained about this job he felt trapped in, a job she'd forced him to get. He told Janet about the affair.

He delivered his monologue about their marriage with such conviction that for a minute the bastard even made Janet wonder if it *had* been her fault. The Janet he described sure sounded like the one to blame. The pieces of his story fit together so perfectly—it was so completely airtight—that at first she didn't notice that this life he was describing, one she'd thought they'd been sharing, was almost completely unrecognizable to her. With the suddenness of an earthquake her idea of their life together crumbled. They'd been living two different marriages. Also like an earthquake, the aftershocks came without warning and for a long time after.

They did what you do. He moved out; temporarily, they said. They went to therapy, got a babysitter so they could spend time alone together. They tried to be honest with each other. As if that was something a husband and wife should have to *try* to do. Eventually Janet managed to dig some hope out of the rubble of their marriage that they might recover, that their family might survive.

During couples therapy one day, she asked almost offhand what department the woman had been transferred to. Why had she asked? So she could warn the new manager's wife? (As if her husband had been the victim of some relentless gold digger.) Out of some vindictive hope that she'd been fired? Janet didn't know why. It popped into her head, and she had to know. It turned out, not only had her ex broken his promise to have the woman transferred, he hadn't even stopped fucking her. They both pretended it was his betrayal, his series of betrayals, that had destroyed their love.

But maybe there had never really been any love to destroy.

"And there they are—it's recorded, but it's still there, right in front of their eyes." The man's story was interminable. "They're checking the details, making sure none of the eyewitness accounts were contaminated." This guy with his contamination. Before Molly came down yesterday morning, Janet and Steve had to listen to a lecture, with this man drilling them for twenty minutes about how they couldn't interfere with Molly's interview, how any influence at all would contaminate the process, ruining the results, destroying any chance of dealing successfully with the creature. How lives were potentially at risk, not to mention all the wasted effort, not just on their parts, the bestiagraphers, but for Steve and Janet and their family as well. But not once in those twenty minutes had he mentioned what kind of effect the presence of these strangers would have on her family. Talk about contamination. Talk about risk—they were putting her whole marriage at risk. "They're even confirming the spelling of the name—*platypus*—yep, it's right. Everything's right, but still this creature's coming at them."

When her ex had said all those times—so many times!—it was just her imagination, he was right. But it wasn't his betrayal she'd been imagining, it was their love. It was him. When her ex finally described the life he'd been living with her, with their daughter, when she understood the gap between his version and hers, she couldn't help but see that she was just as deluded as he was. Where she'd seen love, he'd felt obligation. When she'd felt joy, he'd suffered boredom. All that time she'd been secure, he'd been anxious and stressed and put-upon. Every good feeling she'd had for this man, every happiness she shared with him, had all been imaginary. Imaginary because the man she felt this way toward, the man she shared these feelings with, didn't exist. And perhaps even worse than all of that, she was afraid she was doing it again with Steve.

She'd only managed to escape the depression and despair by convincing herself that her ex's charm or her naiveté or some combination of the two had made her see something that wasn't really there. She'd concluded that the pain and the doubt of her breakup had temporarily shaken her natural confidence in herself and her ability to love, and that Steve's kindness and compassion had restored them to her. Only now did she consider that it might be the other way around. Maybe what was real, what was permanent, was doubt and loneliness. What if confidence and love were never anything but temporary, always something imagined?

It wasn't that she'd married the same kind of man again. Steve wouldn't cheat. Even past her fear she could see that. This was a man who had given sponge baths to his dying wife, who tried so hard to be a good father to Zach, the poor motherless kid. In a marriage like this, a second marriage, you accept, along with your partner, the life they've lived before you met. You just had to. Steve had lived his life, she'd lived hers, and now they were together. For her, it was as if everything that came before had been leading her to the happiness she felt with Steve. Like destiny, or fate, or the plot of a romantic comedy. But how could it possibly be the same for him? His first marriage hadn't been a mistake. No matter how long they were married, how much love she thought they shared, even if they had a child together, how could she ever stop wondering if Steve would always love his first, lost love more? For Janet, Steve was something like a savior. For him, maybe she was a solid plan b. Once again she feared marriage was an imaginary rope bridge built over a very real chasm, and she couldn't help but look down.

"But no one had said anything about poison, and it turns out these things are poisonous. And not only that, but the poison is unbelievably painful. We lost a man down there, one of only about sixty we've lost in the past, I don't know, three-hundred years. Before that, of course, losing men was more common. Back in the heroic age. But now, to lose a man is rare. Or a woman," the man corrected himself, "obviously."

How had she ever thought this Frankenstein family could work? The doubt had started coming late at night, Janet waking in a strange bed certain she'd made the worst mistake she could have possibly made, had put herself, and even worse, Molly, in terrible danger. But then she'd lie there, feel Steve beside her, remember how gentle his love was, how careful he'd been with her, and convince herself she was wrong. And how badly she wanted to be wrong! But those midnight realizations shook something loose. During the days she was with Molly, when it was just the two of them, the bond between them overwhelmed her. Here was real love, impossible to doubt. A love with no room for gaps. Why had she ever thought she needed more than that?

And when Molly started to be afraid—after Zach told her about the monster—all Janet wanted to do was bring Molly into her bed so she could know, with the certainty a child only ever has in her mother, that everything would be fine. And she couldn't do that, because she had this man in her bed, a man who made her believe it was safe to love him.

If this situation with the monster wasn't resolved quickly, this marriage would fall apart, Molly and Janet would be thrust once again into chaos, and Janet would never trust a man again. Would never trust herself to trust a man again. But everything they were going through to get rid of it was making the conclusion ever harder to avoid that not only had Janet trusted too quickly, she'd been unconscionably selfish to get involved with Steve—with any man—in the first place.

"The thing was, the description had been so crazy, they never even considered the possibility that it could be real. This strange hybrid pasted together from pieces of different creatures turned out in the end to be real. But finding that out, people got hurt. Finding that out, a man lost his life."

4. Steve: Thursday Evening

Steve pulled the admittedly beautiful edition of *Grimm's Fairy Tales* down from the top bookshelf in Molly's room. It had been a gift from her paternal grandmother. He hadn't heard much about Janet's first husband's parents but assumed they had never actually read the book or they would have known how inappropriate these stories were for children Molly's age. They were morbid and grotesque and guaranteed to produce nightmares. It was only the absurdity of the situation they found themselves in that made him take it out tonight.

At least every other night for the last three weeks, Molly had cried out that this bogeyman was coming, and each time, the relationship between him and his wife, between his wife and his son, felt the strain. Finally they were doing something about it—bringing in a couple of professionals—and Molly slept soundly two consecutive nights for the first time in almost a month. The hope was that hearing the fairy tale would prevent a third, and Steve was the one who had to read it to her.

Until ten minutes ago, Steve thought he'd be able to convince Janet to be the reader; that he couldn't do it proved how tenuous things were. It was just the latest in a series of discussions, arguments, and fights, but it was the first time Janet literally would not listen to what he was saying. Their disagreements had become heated before, but at least they'd always heard each other out. Tonight,

Janet simply refused. First she refused to read the story, then she refused to engage at all. When he stopped trying to talk to her, he had no idea what his wife even wanted. Did she want *him* to read Molly the story? Did she not want *anyone* to read Molly the story? Did she want to kick the bestiagraphers out of the house altogether?

So Steve made the decision himself. They'd come too far to kick the bestiagraphers out. All the anxiety of the last two nights, all the frustration, might be sunk costs, but even if kicking them out could get things back to the way they'd been three days ago—and he doubted that was possible at this point—he didn't know if they'd make it anyway. As a couple. As a family. Three days ago, they'd been in a state of slightly less rapid disintegration, not equilibrium. The only way out was through, so in spite of every paternal instinct he had, he read Molly the story of Bluebeard.

He kissed her on the forehead and wiped away her tears when he finished, then sat with her while she calmed down. Before he closed the door on his way out, Molly said, sniffling, "Are they coming again tonight?"

Except for not telling her what a scumbag her father was, he'd never lied to the girl, but tonight he felt he had to. "No sweetie, they got just what they needed."

"Really?"

"Really Tiger, you did great."

Molly's smile was a small reward for his treachery. He waited at the door for a bit after he closed it, then went downstairs, past Zach asleep on the couch, to the kitchen. His wife was busy making coffee and putting out dishes, so he phoned the bestiagraphers from the den where Molly wouldn't hear him.

When he went back to the kitchen, Janet was sitting at

the table pouring vodka into a short glass full of ice. Steve did what was supposed to be a comical double-take and said in a thick Eastern European accent, "Vell Meester Bond . . ." She motioned to the glass next to her. "Please," he said, and she poured him one.

Maybe she didn't remember telling him that vodka on the rocks was what she used to drink with her ex and maybe she did. Either way, he took it as a shot across the bow. As if he needed another warning. She and her ex had been poor, the way everyone's poor at that age, and they drank the cheapest vodka they could find while they imagined their future together. For Steve and his first wife, it had been Chilean red wine, the only kind they could afford in sufficient quantity. With other couples, it was tequila or rum or gin or weed. It didn't matter. When you meet someone at a certain point in your life, and he or she is at the same point, when the future is uncertain and that uncertainty hasn't yet become more terrifying than exciting, and it feels as if no one's ever gone through what you two are about to go through together, it creates something that even death or betrayal can't erase. You get loaded and you think about the future, and you're young but feel mature, and maybe you're having sex regularly for the first time but even if that's not the case it's the first time you've had that kind of sex, and even though you have no idea while you're in it, you're creating something outside time, an enchanted place you can go back to if you get the incantation right, a place that links your present self with that past self, your past with the present of all the young people going through it right now, and with your kids, who'll go through it themselves one day. So Janet was practicing the incantation. It didn't look as if it was working, and he couldn't help, so he took his drink into the living room to wait for the bestiagraphers, who were staying in a motel a few minutes away.

Zach was sprawled on the couch, asleep in front of the TV. The kid even slept with a sneer. Steve scolded himself; that wasn't fair. It wasn't always this way. When Steve's first wife told him she was pregnant, it was the culmination of these flashes of potency he'd felt throughout his life, times when he'd kissed a beautiful girl for the first time, stood up to someone bigger and stronger, hit a homerun. He had found a woman to love, they had created this life together, and Steve would provide for the health and happiness of both of them. He expected that once he achieved that feeling, it would never go away. As soon as Zach was born, though, the first time he held his son in his arms, a new and desperate love exploded within him that brought with it the sudden understanding that he wasn't in charge anymore, that even if he was still at the wheel of his own life, someone else was working the accelerator, and there weren't any brakes.

But of course, when you live with a feeling long enough, you stop noticing it. Things you know are forgotten. They don't always stay forgotten. For nearly a year, he watched his wife's body weaken, and then her mind, until everything he recognized as her was gone. Even just making a quick phone call in the den where she'd spent her last months had brought back the despair. Despair for her, despair at his utter powerlessness in the face of her disease. His most exhaustive and exhausting efforts to comfort her had done so little when compared to her pain, weakness, and depression as to be unnoticeable. Not unnoticeable as much as laughable, if that were possible. It was as if all he could do to ease her passing was make her understand that he and their son would never recover from the loss of her, and what kind of comfort is that to a mother?

He didn't know what recovering even meant, but he continued living and had come to love Janet. He'd thought she loved him back. But the way something as common as a bogeyman in Molly's closet had threatened their relationship, despite his every effort to keep it together, forced him to question what it was based on in the first place. That he was surprised in the face of this new failure, he could only take as proof of his continuing inability to acknowledge his own impotence.

The bestiagraphers pulled up in their rented car, relieving Steve of his thoughts. He opened the front door so they wouldn't knock and went out to help them carry their equipment in, though it was no more than they could handle themselves. When he came back in with the small black bag holding the speaker, Zach was awake and looking around in confusion. He saw the bestiagraphers and looked embarrassed to be caught sleeping. Or guilty, as if he were letting Molly down by sleeping on the job.

They arranged themselves in the kitchen. Janet poured the coffee, the man set up the laptop and speaker, the woman spread her notes on the table. Steve looked for a way to be helpful and failed to find one. No words were wasted. The tension between the partners was obvious, as he assumed was that between him and his wife.

He'd slept maybe five hours the last two nights combined but went to work anyway. He just had to get away from Janet. For her sake as much as his. Everything he did was wrong. This morning, he'd let Janet sleep in and got the kids ready for school himself, but he'd fed Molly the sugary cereal Zach ate. When he tried to tell Janet one breakfast wasn't such a big deal, what she heard was him saying she was too hard on the kids, too inflexible with her rules. He made her feel as if they weren't in this together. And so it went, no attempt to help was executed well enough, no comment was innocent enough, not to make things worse.

Zach came into the kitchen completely exhausted. He was a wreck. Steve and Janet had both told him he should go to bed, but the closest he got was a nap on the couch. He admitted at dinner that he'd fallen asleep in earth science that day, and he would've fallen asleep again in algebra if his teacher hadn't embarrassed him in front of the class. The only person getting any sleep was Molly. There was a strange comfort in that, the fact that Molly could sleep despite everything. A few days ago, he would've mentioned this to Janet, to encourage her that they were doing all right considering, but now he was afraid how she might take it.

Just as they had the last two nights, everyone listened when they turned the speaker on, and like the last two nights, what they heard was Molly rolling over a few times, dropping her moose, picking up her moose, and eventually falling asleep. Reading the fairy tale had done nothing but make Steve feel cruel.

"I was sure," the woman said, "that after talking about the creature all day it would have shown up that first night."

"Or, barring that, the second night, after we went over the details and showed her the sketch," the man said. They were trying to justify themselves to Steve and Janet, maybe to each other.

"The problem is," the man said, "she's too good a sleeper."

"If you had kids," Janet said, "you'd know there's no

such thing as too good a sleeper."

"What she means—" Steve began.

"I said what I meant."

It was as if Steve couldn't help himself. He looked at his wife with the hope of showing he was sorry, but all he managed to do was grimace. Janet got up to refill the ice in her glass and asked if anyone needed anything. No one did.

Everyone settled into their work—the man on the computer, the woman with her notes, both at the table. Zach sat on a stool at the counter doing his homework, sighing even louder than usual. Janet was leaning against the sink sipping her vodka, and Steve wandered the center of the room, pacing around like a sheepdog with a scattered flock. He sat down at the table hoping his wife would sit next to him. She did not.

After several more minutes of tense almost-silence, Zach threw down his pencil. It bounced off the granite counter and rolled across the floor. "Why isn't it coming?"

As if Zach's words could make it appear, everyone looked at the speaker. Janet was about to say something, and Steve just hoped she didn't yell at his son. The woman spoke first.

"What we think is that it's because she's asleep. If one of Molly's defenses against the creature is to pretend she's asleep, then actually being asleep should prevent it from coming also."

"So what do we do?" Steve asked. "Pack up all the equipment and forget about it?" He'd said it to point out how ridiculous the idea was, but Janet's face showed she didn't think it was ridiculous at all.

"We wake her," the man said.

"Come on," Steve said. "Real or not, she's terrified of

that thing. She's sleeping peacefully for chrissakes."

The woman was trying to change Steve's mind with an empathetic look.

"I could do it," Zach said quietly. "I mean . . ."

Janet shook her head. The man looked on blankly. The woman shifted her empathetic gaze to Zach. After thirty seconds, Zach took the woman's appeal and the lack of verbal objection from anyone else as assent. He took a loud deep breath and left the room.

Everyone still in the kitchen listened to Zach's approach through the speaker. First, all they heard was Molly's sleepy breathing, then, barely, Zach's soft footfalls in the hallway. The door opened and swept over the carpet. Zach's footsteps got louder as he crossed to Molly's bed. She stirred; the mattress springs creaked under the weight of Zach's body. He whispered something they couldn't make out. Then again. Molly, sleepily, said, "What?"

"Molls," Zach said. "I just wanted to see how you were. The monster hasn't come, huh?"

"No," Molly said, but the way she said it meant "not yet."

"I don't think it will," Zach said. "I think it's gone."

What was he doing? Janet, whose patience for Zach was long gone, looked at Steve as if he ought to keep his damn son in line. Steve could almost hear Molly smile at her brother, and once again was amazed at the bond they'd developed, so much more secure than their parents'.

"Forever?" Molly asked, happiness in her voice. "Are you sure?"

"Yeah," Zach said. "Well, I'm not *sure*. But I hope so."

The professionals immediately understood what Zach did. It took Steve a moment longer. Janet was furious.

Zach said goodnight, left the room, and came down to the kitchen. Molly didn't fall back asleep.

Molly, miracle that she was, had almost immediately broken through Zach's withdrawal and sarcasm. When she and Janet moved in, Zach surrendered his bedroom with minimal nudging. Steve guessed Zach wanted to be a martyr—the bedroom he'd be moving into was smaller, less insulated, and too sunny in the morning for a teenager's schedule. But Molly had involved Zach in every aspect of the room's interior design and had offered so often to take the smaller room—since, as she said, she was smaller—that she won Zach over. Occasionally this affection and tenderness he had for Molly would make Zach blush self-consciously or try to avoid her, and Steve wanted to hug him and tell him he understood what Zach was feeling. But, as much as he hated to admit this, Steve was afraid Zach would shrug him off or, maybe even worse, change out of either embarrassment or spite. Zach was always ashamed of his best qualities, and it broke Steve's heart.

Zach sat in the kitchen looking as if he wasn't sure he'd done the right thing. The rest of them listened to Molly's small, scared noises through the speaker. It was obscene. Then something changed in Molly's voice and the two women leaned in toward the speaker. The men leaned in a moment after. Zach shrunk away.

One long *mom* preceded the ratatat of *dad dad dad dad dad,* and the partners launched up the stairs. Steve followed with Janet behind him.

The woman listened at Molly's door while the man stood in Steve's way.

"Molly, honey, what's going on?" the woman said. It should've been Steve or Janet asking, not this stranger.

"IT'S HERE IT'S HERE IT'S HERE," came back through the door.

The woman turned a couple of pages in her notebook and nodded to her partner to open the door. When he did, she rushed straight to the small slatted doors of the crawlspace. Steve ran to the bed, scooped Molly in his arms, and swept her down to the kitchen. Janet tried to soothe Molly as they ran.

Steve sat at the table and held Molly in his lap. Her head rested in the crook of his right elbow, and Janet leaned over them with her hands on Molly's cheeks. Zach, struggling not to sound like he was crying, kept telling Molly she was all right, but Molly in her fear and shock was sobbing too loud to hear anything. Janet, crying as well, took her daughter from Steve, turned away from Steve and Zach, and squeezed Molly tight to her chest.

Through the speaker came the sound of the slatted doors crashing open, then a crescendo of angry noise that had both the growl of the world's most threatening dog and the roar of a jet engine in it. Terse questions between the partners emerged from out of the noise: "What's going on?" "Something's wrong." "Why isn't the—?" Then the man saying, "Check the details! Every detail!"

Zach let out a groan. Molly was howling in terror at the sounds coming through the speaker. Steve tried to shut it off but couldn't figure out how.

"I don't understand," the woman said.

"Why is it—?" the man said. Then he screamed in pain. "Aah! My leg. It bit me. Jesus, they're like razors."

Steve ripped the speaker wire from the computer and ran back up the stairs. The partners had to scream to be heard over the noise.

"Leave me," the man said to his partner, "just find out

what's wrong."

Steve burst through the door, and the roar came alive around him, as if the air itself was wailing in agony. "What's that?" he shouted. "That's not—"

"It is," the man said. "Go! We have to get out."

Coming out of the crawlspace was no bogeyman. This was a monster, and Steve knew every bit of Molly's fear. What had sounded like a cartoon when she described it was the embodiment of terror to gaze upon. The thing was the same color as his wife's lifeless eyes the moment after she died. Its skin was slick, and under that skin it was inchoate and bloated. There was no indication of a skeleton, and its muscles had no definition to them. It seemed to be creating itself before his eyes, like a Polaroid developing. Because it was not quite formed, he couldn't tell how big it was. He did know it was too large to fit in the crawlspace, and yet there it was, coming through the doors. It stood on only three legs, had an enormous head on top of a neck that should have been too long and thin to hold it up. Its defiance of gravity, its disregard of physics, was one more terror. Its eyes were empty, its nose bulbous and malformed, oozing snot or pus. Its enormous mouth was full of hundreds of teeth arranged in rows, each one a perfect triangle with a dagger's tip. Steve was paralyzed in the face of the creature. In the face of pure fear.

The man had been talking to Steve, but only now did Steve notice. The man was limping toward the door, saying, "Come on! We have to get out." But he was too slow with his injury, would never make it before the monster caught him. Steve remembered what Molly had said about protecting herself.

"Go! I'll use the blanket," Steve said and ripped the

comforter off Molly's bed. He held it between the creature and the door while the bestiagraphers made their escape. His first thought had been to get out as well, but he didn't. He stayed and battled the monster. He couldn't see it behind the blanket, nor could he hear exactly where it was—the noise was everywhere—but he moved by instinct, guided by something outside himself, turning with the blanket, cutting off where he knew the monster wanted to go. The monster couldn't touch him through the barrier, yet he could sense its frustration as he maneuvered it ever closer to the small slatted doors it had come through. He caught glimpses of its sponge-like feet below the blanket, heard their squishing, like walking in thick, wet socks. He saw glimpses of the monster's oozing nose, its shark teeth, coming around the edge of the comforter. But Steve moved the blanket as if he'd trained for years to use it like this, blocking its every move, imposing his will on it. When the noise rose in pitch and volume, when the windows started shaking and books fell off the shelves, Steve knew he would win. He forced the monster back into the crawlspace, and when it was all the way inside, he slammed the slatted doors shut and fastened them with the purple scrunchie. The noise died. Steve knelt on the ground holding the comforter.

He slumped against Molly's bed. For the first time in far too long, he wanted to talk to his wife, to tell her what he'd been through with no fear he'd be misunderstood. He felt like a boy who wanted to explain how he scored the winning touchdown, detail every movement, relive in words the thoughtless joy of action. He stood up and turned away from the small doors.

As he followed the drops of blood left by the limping man, he thought about how he would describe it. At first, he compared it to bullfighting, but that wasn't right. Bullfighting had something passive and indirect about it, avoiding the bull and darting it as it passed. If the encounter with the monster hadn't been so dangerous, he would have described it as a dance, an aggressive dance like the tango, an assertion of will and grace and strength. But really, he'd felt like the tide, flowing this way and that, fluid yet forceful, instinctual and overwhelming.

When he got to the kitchen, he saw that he would not be reliving his victory. At the sight of blood, Molly was crying even harder than before. The woman pressed a kitchen towel to the man's wound. Janet held her daughter. It looked as if Janet and Zach had exchanged words, and Zach was fighting off tears and slouching as if he might disappear into the chair.

The partners were beaten. The woman pulled the towel away from the wound and inspected her partner's leg. "We have to get you to the infirmary," she said. Then she turned to Janet. "I'll submit our report, and the Society will decide where to take it from here. They'll be in touch with you." She helped her partner stand. "Someone will be by to pick up our equipment."

Steve waited for her to continue, but when she didn't, asked, "What happened?"

The woman looked at Janet and at Zach before looking at Steve. "There was a discrepancy in the details, which usually means contamination. Someone will be in touch after they review our report. They'll be able to explain and offer you some options. I suggest you keep Molly out of that room for now."

The man leaned on his partner and the two bestiagraphers made their way to the door. Steve looked to Janet for an explanation, but though she looked back at him, there was no familiarity in it, no warmth. Zach wouldn't even make eye contact.

5. Steve: Thursday Late Night

Steve woke when he kicked the armrest of the couch trying to stretch his legs. His wife was in the den, moaning in pain. He sat up to go to her. His wife wasn't in the den. His wife was gone. His body shuddered in a bitter snort. He had a new wife, and she was in his bed with her daughter. Steve was sleeping on the couch. Just for now. Until Molly wasn't afraid anymore.

He'd heard it, though, his first wife saying, "It's bad. Bad." About the pain. He must have dreamt it. He put his elbows on his knees and dropped his head, surrendering to the heaviness. His back and neck muscles lengthened, and it felt good, the ache in his muscles, to stretch after sleeping hunched up on the couch, after living with so much tension.

"Dad?"

His shoulder muscles clenched. He looked up to see Zach on the stairway. In the dark he couldn't make out his son's expression, but he saw by his posture, the way he seemed to be leaning away, that he was afraid to come down. Was that what it meant? Afraid? Jesus, he was out of practice.

"What's up?" Steve said, and flicked his head to let Zach know he could come sit on the couch. Steve moved his blanket to make room.

"I can't sleep," Zach said before he sat down.

"Yeah."

"Sorry I woke you." Zach sat down where Steve patted the couch next to him.

"I wasn't sleeping well. Bad dream."

"You have nightmares?"

Steve hesitated. "About your mom."

"Oh," Zach said. "I miss her."

"Yeah. Me too."

Zach seemed to be weighing whether Steve was just saying that to agree with him or if he really meant it.

"We never talk about her," Zach finally said.

"I was afraid it would . . ."

Zach nodded. "Me too. I guess."

"Maybe let's stop doing that."

They sat in silence, each waiting for the other to start. Zach finally said, "Janet hates me." His voice cracked at the word 'hates,' and a tremor ran through his body, but he didn't cry.

"Zach," Steve said. "She doesn't hate you." He slid a little closer to his son, put his hand on his knee.

"Of course she does. Look what I did." Zach couldn't keep himself from crying this time, and once he started, it took over. It was a pitiful sight, Zach helpless to stop the tears and the snot and the bestial grunting, which reminded Steve of a noise the monster made a few hours ago. A defeated sound. Zach's guard was completely down; even yesterday, he would not have cried like this in front of Steve. Not even when his mother died.

Steve put his arm around Zach's head and pulled him close. His son's tears dampened his neck. He shook in harmony with his son's quaking body.

"Oh . . . Zach," Steve said. He wanted a term of endearment, to call him 'honey' or 'sweetheart' or something, some word that would let his son know how he felt, how profound his love was, and his sympathy, but there was no word they used that would do that. "Zach, she knows you didn't mean it."

"I did mean it. I wanted them to fail. To protect Molly. I thought . . ."

"Oh," Steve said and found that after everything that had happened, there was still a further emptiness, another, deeper bottom. For god's sake, where does it end? His own pain and hurt and struggle weren't enough, now he had to witness this, this unbearable sadness and guilt in his son?

He pulled Zach even tighter, kissed him roughly on the head. Even while he did it, he wondered how long it had been since Zach had let himself be held like this, since his son had given himself over to being cared for. When was the last time Steve had tried?

With nothing else to say, Steve just repeated, "Zach, it's okay. It's going to be okay."

What could he explain? That he suspected Zach had in some way done Janet a favor, giving her the perfect excuse to pull away from her husband and stepson, giving her a more immediate problem—her daughter's terror—that would put off indefinitely, perhaps forever, the hard and uncertain work of trying to save her marriage?

Should he explain that no matter what Zach had done or not done, Steve and Janet's marriage might have been doomed anyway, explain to him now, before he got hurt again, that loving someone means eventually discovering you are completely powerless in the face of their pain and fear? Or was it better to let Zach feel the crushing weight of responsibility for Steve sleeping on the couch, for the coldness that would enter their home, for the eventual severing of this brief family into the two half-families from which it had formed, just so Zach could live a few more years with the illusion that what he did mattered?

Steve wanted to laugh, not because it was funny, but because he knew even this choice didn't matter. Whatever he said, however convincingly, Zach wouldn't learn the lesson until life forced him to, and even then—if Steve was any guide—he'd have to learn it again and again and again.

So he didn't say anything but his son's name and didn't do anything but hold him close. He hoped against reason that he was wrong, that Zach's lessons wouldn't always be so hard, that Janet's withdrawal was only temporary, that this family could be saved. Maybe, if he tried as hard as he could, he could imagine that: His wife opening herself again to him, to Zach; his son having an easier time of things, talking through his pain with a therapist, with Steve, maybe one day even finding that his sensitivity was something someone loved about him, instead of it being a weakness, something to be mocked, something to hide. Maybe they could imagine this family into existence again. And Steve would try, he would, because even though pain and death and fear had won so far—even though they would probably always win—stupid, blind, impotent love would never stop trying.

BEYOND DEFIANCE

Alison Foster

BEYOND DEFIANCE

Alison Foster

It is my turn to drive.

We are half way between Las Vegas and Albuquerque. The road stretches out in front of us for miles. Endless. Flat. So very flat.

Sam and I are on our first road trip together. Our relationship is brand new. Still in the discovery stage. There is much we don't know about each other yet. And Sam hasn't done anything to annoy me. So far, so good.

I have rented a car. A subcompact. At the time I didn't know what that meant. I thought small, inexpensive. It turns out to be a toy car like the kind the clowns drive in the circus when twenty of them come tumbling out to a tent full of laughter. Well, this car is funny, too. It is aptly named a Ford Aspire. Sam is tall, well over six feet, and he is jammed and crammed into the driver's seat. His legs barely squeeze in under the steering wheel. But Sam doesn't seem to mind. He hasn't grumbled or told me how stupid I am for ordering such a ridiculous car. Instead, he makes a joke out of it. He says, "Our little toy car aspires to be a real car." I laugh. It is our first private joke together.

We spent one night in Las Vegas, but neither of us had

liked the place very much. Too neon, too smoky, and too crowded. We played the nickel slots and were okay with losing our money slowly, not all at once. We left our hotel on the strip right after breakfast, aiming to make it to Albuquerque before dark. Looking at the unfolded map in my lap, the expanse seems possible. I estimate eight hours.

When we stop for lunch at an unpretentious Mexican cafe tucked away off the highway,

Sam is respectful to the waitress. His table manners are respectable, and he doesn't chew food with his mouth open. We each order a margarita. No salt. Something we have in common. I am taking notes. Not four beers like my husband before him. Sam pays for lunch and leaves a tip, a good one.

After lunch, Sam drives for a couple more hours. Still no complaints. He says he loves to drive. We watch as the terrain grows horizontal and more desolate.

We pull into the first gas station we have seen in miles at a town called Defiance. I chuckle to myself. What a great name. I could live here. But I couldn't really; we are too far from anywhere. I gaze at the chips and the candy bars but pay for two bottles of water. We walk back to the car, across the hot cement. We are alone except for the attendant inside the unairconditioned booth.

Sam asks, "You wanna drive?"

I have been dreading this moment. I am from New York City and not much of a driver.

My parents don't even own a car. I didn't learn to drive until my junior year in college. But fair is fair. It is my turn. I don't want Sam to think I am inept or helpless. I am pretty sure he has signed on for a capable and independent woman. Knowing how to drive a car falls under this category.

With what I hope is a convincing nod, I slide behind the wheel, find the lever to move the seat forward, adjust the side and rear-view mirrors, and snap on the seatbelt. I feel my shirt begin to stick to my back. My face grows flush and my hands are trembling. I dig through my overstuffed purse for my sunglasses. I go over the steps in my head. All I have to do is get on the highway and go straight. So first, put the key into the ignition. Check. Put the car into gear. Check. Foot on and then off the brake. I am bold. I am defiant. *I can do this.*

I ask Sam, "Should we get gas; do we need to fill up?" He will think I'm stalling. He has already kicked off his sneakers. He is settling into the passenger seat.

"Nah, we should be good. This engine is pretty small." Ha, ha. He has noticed the diminutive size of the car.

I slowly pull away from the station and head for the highway. The little car shakes slightly as I continue to build up speed. I expertly glide in front of a huge semi-truck, and we don't get sucked under the wheels. We don't die. Check.

Look at me. I'm a professional driver. I place my hands correctly on the steering wheel at ten and two. I check the rear-view mirror. Look at me. I am driving in New Mexico with my gorgeous new man. I am free. My two children are home with their father, my ex-husband. I haven't been away from them since the divorce. I check the speedometer. Maybe there is something on the radio? There is no other way to listen to music. With the window rolled down, the warm air blows across my face. I even dare to take my eyes off the road for a second to notice the dry, desert scenery whizzing by. With my left elbow resting on the windowsill, I wonder if I will get a tan.

Should I roll up my t-shirt sleeve?

KA-CHUNK.

What the hell is that? Am I going too fast for our little Aspire? I check the dashboard. No warning lights. But there it is again. KA-CHUNK. The car is beginning to slow down and tremble.

"I think you better pull over." Sam says calmly. What have I done? I ease up on the gas pedal and somehow make it over to the shoulder. The car stops running all together.

I wait for Sam to yell at me, our idyllic vacation spoiled. Our relaxing retreat ruined.

Sam is putting on his shoes.

"Where are you going?"

"To get gas. We ran out of gas, that's all." Where's the drama in that? The blaming, the name calling. Nothing. I wait. We are in the middle of nowhere, miles from a pay phone or another gas station. We haven't passed a town since I started driving twenty minutes ago. And it's beginning to grow dark. The temperature is dropping and the shadows from an occasional car roaring by grow longer. Pretty soon there will be no light at all.

Sam says, "There's got to be an exit up ahead. You stay with the car, okay?" Sam walks over to the edge of the highway and sticks out his thumb. The trucks are going by so fast I don't see how they can stop even if they want to. But in seconds a sports car skids to a stop a few feet ahead of us spraying gravel. Sam sprints up to the red convertible and waves to me. "Don't go anywhere." And just like that I am alone. Again. Just me and the tumbleweed or sagebrush or whatever the vegetation is out here.

I remain in the driver's seat. Maybe I can read. But the

bright white glow from the overhead light shines down on me like a spotlight on a stage. I've seen this movie before. I know what happens to a woman abandoned by the side of the road. Searchers will find my body weeks from now, my dismembered foot partially exposed under the sparse vegetation. Sam will identify me by the lone black Birkenstock. I can't decide whether I am better off inside or outside. I am afraid a coyote will eat me; I am way too visible outside of the car. No bush or tree to tuck behind. So I sit in the dark as the trucks whoosh by and shake the miniature car. I have to pee. I have been alone for well over an hour; it is lightless. No sun, no moon.

Headlights way far away come straight towards me. The two bright lights shine directly and illuminate the inside of the car. My body is fully visible. Oh God, please be Sam. The car coming at me slows down.

Sam unfolds his long legs from the passenger seat of a red Mustang, the same car that stopped for Sam before. With a shiny gas can in hand, Sam thanks the young guy who has driven way out of his way to help us. He couldn't be more than nineteen. I thank him. He says, "Just paying it forward, Ma'am." Oh God, I don't look that old do I? He tells me, he is heading to Iraq tomorrow. Last week he ran out of gas and someone stopped to help him. I am clearly no longer in New York.

Sam gets behind the wheel. The engine sputters awake. My driving stint is over. Sam and

I have barely spoken. He checks in.

"You okay?"

"Yup, all good. You?"

"Yup." Not angry. Not mad. Just is.

We drive past a sign, and I see where I have been. Waiting. Trusting. Thoreau, New Mexico. No pond, no woods. I have been alone in nature, not quite a religious experience, but a spiritual adventure of sorts. A detoxing from my old life.

All good.

AN INCOMPLETE LIST OF MY RODENT QUALITIES, AS COMPILED BY MY EX-BOYFRIEND WHEN HE STILL LOVED ME

Jasmine Sawers

AN INCOMPLETE LIST OF MY RODENT QUALITIES, AS COMPILED BY MY EX-BOYFRIEND WHEN HE STILL LOVED ME

Jasmine Sawyers

2. How I am fuzzy and round.

17. How I fit into convenient shirt pockets.

84. How I will hoard food in my cheeks for later.

112. How I clasp my hands before my chest in supplication.

113. How like a person's those hands are.

132. How I will climb the same wires again and again, fall on my tiny skull again and again, look up and think "that seems like a good idea" again and again and again and again.

146. How no amount of light food and running in my wheel will result in weight loss.

158. How public my bowel movements are.

170. How I burrow into the bedding until no light can shine through.

201. How I stare and stare.

274. How I skitter from his hands.

299. How I will accept a sunflower seed so gently.

300. How I show contempt for yogurt drops.

301. How I bite, just a little.

460. How filthy the floor of my cage is.

483. How the slightest change in interior design disrupts my habitual nature so much that I can't find the water.

500. How surprised and perturbed I am by the presence of cats.

521. How I eat my young.

522. How it is better if I am housed by myself.

540. How I always shit where I eat.

625. How I gnaw at the bars.

639. How I will make my triumphant escape only to find myself underneath the refrigerator and in need of rescue.

650. How I will never love him back.

664. How nubby my tail is.

677. How, when I die, I will be alone and left to rot until someone notices the smell and calls a strapping young man to put me in a garbage bag and leave me in the dumpster.

694. How I cringe from the light.

SOFT AND SPOKEN

Rachel Brittain

SOFT AND SPOKEN

Rachel Brittain

The calico-bush grew wild and free in the woods around the still, though they had long since shed their pretty pink-speckled flowers in favor of coffee-brown pods of cocooned fruit. Low-lying brush crunched under Lena's boots as she and her sister trudged up the slope to the backyard distillery their father operated in the woods behind their house.

After school, and the daily routine of their more normal chores, like sweeping the porch and making sure the cats were still there and fed, Lena and Isa were expected to do their part for the family business. Picking up hog meal from town, mixing the mash, cleaning the still, or, like today, going out back to help their daddy with a finished batch.

Moonshining was serious business, as he always liked to remind them.

Lena and Isa carried two pails each, ready to cart the fresh liquor back to the house where they'd bottle it up in old glass mason jars, jugs, and empty beer bottles saved up just for that purpose. Lena kicked at the edges of the overgrown path while Isa swung her pails in time to some internal beat as they walked.

One of Isa's pails struck Lena's with a shrieking metallic clank. *Watch it,* Lena scolded—an older sister's prerogative—even if they were too far away from even their closest neighbor for anybody but their father to hear.

Isa ignored her—a younger sister's prerogative—sticking out her tongue and going right back to swinging.

It's not me he's gonna yell at if we get caught being noisy, said Lena.

Not that they would—get caught, that is. They lived a long way out and anyway everybody knew what they were doing out here. Half the town got their liquor from the Larkins, and nobody except maybe the sheriff would want to do anything about it. Assuming the sheriff didn't just want a few bottles of his own.

Something daddy always liked to say: *Moonshiners don't go to prison for moonshining; they go to prison for tax evasion.* Which was usually followed by an exclamation, something like, *damn regulation,* or *federal theft, that's what it is, girls, don't never trust the government.*

They cleared the hill and trudged the rest of the way into the little, overgrown clearing where the still was set up.

The large, copper still was so hot the air shimmered around it, the propane furnace beneath it cranked up to full. Lena knew this contraption like the back of her hand—better even, because dusty brown freckles appeared there sometimes where they hadn't been before, and the still was always the same.

The copper coil snaking out of the still connected to the thump keg where the steam collected along with the last few bits of solid mash before the rest re-evaporated on its way to the coiled worm pipe and into the worm box full of cold water (collected from the creek just down the hill). The cold finally condensed the alcohol steam back into liquid that dripped in fat drops from the spout and into the bucket.

Theirs' was a large, industrial cleaning bucket—the kind you might find in a janitor's closet or catching a new batch of moonshine, depending on the kind of life you were living. Two others were lined up next to it, red and white like someone was halfway to being patriotic before they decided to heck with it.

Whatever collected there usually got re-filtered through the whole system at least of couple of times. Once through and it wouldn't be nearly strong enough, but put it through a few more times—

Liquor, 150 proof, just like that.

Bill Larkin was tending to the propane tank, moving between it and the catch bucket where the first drips of the crystal clear moonshine were beginning to pool.

Girls, there you are, he said, not even looking up as they approached.

School ran late, Lena said in explanation, even though he hadn't asked—or accused. It was just better to say up front than wait around until explanations became excuses.

He nodded but didn't otherwise acknowledge them. Fine by Lena, who focused on the steady, familiar sound of mash plinking against the bottom of the thump keg. Isa patted the cool edge of the worm box fondly.

The drip slowly collected in the bucket until it created a shallow pool that their daddy threw into the brush over his shoulder. The foreshot—that first bit of almost pure methanol that could make a man go blind or even dead—was as good as poison. He tossed the bucket aside, swapping it out for the red bucket. A few precious drops pooled into a glob of mud on the ground as he lined it up under the open pipe of the condenser.

Lena took the bucket over to the stream and rinsed it out as the cold water numbed her hands. By the time she got back the bucket was already half full. Daddy dipped a finger into the trickle to taste it, before nodding and switching the red bucket out for the final white one.

The red bucket, full of the harsh "heads" would be set aside until the heart of the moonshine was distilled, then returned to fill up with the last, bitter "tails" of the liquor, neither of which should be drunk as-is and both of which would be saved for future spirit runs.

Lena moved the bucket of heads out of the way, breathing carefully through her mouth, though the fumes still sizzled right through to her brain.

As they waited, daddy waved Lena over. *Come here, Magdalena,* he said, *you're old enough, you ought to know how to do this.* He handed her a metal spoon with a rag wrapped around the end and pointed down toward the bucket of clear liquor rippling with a steady drip, drip from the condenser. *Go on, get you a spoonful.*

Lena had seen him do this enough times to know what he was getting at. She scooped up a careful spoonful and held it out in front of her like an offering in the church of the hills.

Good, he said, *Now, you watch this too, Isa. It's important.* He pulled out his lighter and flicked it on, slowly bringing the flame down to the spoon. *Steady, now.*

The flame touched the surface of the moonshine and a wave of fire moved across the surface until the whole thing was ablaze.

Watch the color, now, he said and both girls leaned in closer. *Blue's safe, yellow's bad—just like that.*

They watched the tiny blue tips of the flame licking

against the air in front of Lena, pretending they hadn't watched him do this a hundred times before. 150-proof burned like nobody's business, that was for sure.

And you know the other, he said. *Red means lead, red means dead. You see a red flame, you throw the whole thing out, you understand?*

Lena nodded. They knew. They'd heard enough stories about the dirty radiator coils old moonshiners had sometimes used and the antifreeze and lead poisoning that might kill you, but only if you were lucky. Anyway, they didn't use anything like that. They knew better.

They weren't new to all this. Their family had been moonshiners since back before Prohibition, or so it went according to daddy, and the girls had been helping with the still since they were old enough to hold a bucket, maybe even before.

My knees are sore. Grab me that bucket there, he said, waving toward the freshly cleaned foreshot bucket. Isa went to grab it as Lena watched the last of the flames spend themselves out.

Isa's ungodly shriek made her drop it, heedless of the burning-hot remnants of alcohol.

What, girl, what? their daddy asked, jumping at the noise.

Isa signed the words for *snake* and *gold*—the closest she could get to copper with her piecemeal homesign.

Copperhead, Lena explained, turning to their daddy.

Sure enough, a baby copperhead was curled in the crook of the empty bucket and peering out at them with dark, suspicious eyes.

Isa took a few careful steps back, but, having gotten over the initial surprise of almost grabbing the thing, crouched to peer down at it.

Lena didn't feel so curious or forgiving. She handed her daddy the large, dull-edged shovel he always kept handy and glanced away as he tipped the little snake out of the bucket and brought the shovel down to behead it in one quick, decisive swing. Isa looked on with clinical fascination.

Alright now, everybody's fine, he said as he scooped the head into the shovel, away from the twitching body, and walked over to the edge of the clearing to fling it into the woods, far away from the girls. *Just don't be wandering off that way into the woods, now. That thing'll still snap shut sure as anything, and I don't want anybody getting snakebit.*

We won't, said Lena, and coming from her it was as good as a promise.

The catch bucket was almost full to overflowing in the midst of their distraction, so daddy switched it out and handed it off to the girls who divided it into their buckets, less likely to spill and easier to carry down to the house that way.

Go bottle this up, he told them.

We've got homework, said Lena. Isa rolled her eyes.

He gave her a sour look. *You bottle this up, then you'll have time for whatever else. You think that schoolwork of yours is what pays the bills? No. Pull your weight like we all do.*

School's important too, Lena mumbled, and she didn't even have to see her sister to know that she was silently sending her signals to shut the hell up.

You talking back to me? he snapped. Lena shook her head no. *Better not be.*

She chanced a glance back at her sister and saw her sign, lighting-fast, *hush.*

This here, this is the real world. Just as important as anything they're teaching you in that schoolroom, you got me?

said daddy.

Lena thought that was a whole lot of bull, so she just nodded. Daddy could see it in her eyes, though, and her conspicuous silence, so his eyes squinted tighter down at her.

Magdalena, he said, *I won't say it again. You understand me?*

Yessir, said Lena.

And it wasn't a lie, but Lena couldn't quite bring herself to believe it.

▪ ▪ ▪

The curse was the worst kept secret in town. Everyone knew about it and everyone talked about it—though not, usually, to their faces. The curse—or the rumor of the curse—had several variations, but most of them held at least the ley lines of this truth:

Magdalena and Isadora, the Larkin girls—maybe more often known as Lena and Isa, at least to the people who liked them—were born cursed. The why and how of it were a little trickier, but this one thing was sure.

Gossipmongers around town liked to embellish the more improbable versions involving changeling children left to replace real babies, dangerous fantasy novels detailing satanic rituals, and drinking bad soda. What kind that was, exactly, was up for question.

Their mother, when she had been around, said there was no curse—and not just because she had been implicated in several of the rumors. She was no fridge mother and there was nothing wrong with her babies, whatever anyone said, and that was that. She called them different, or—when she'd been in a particularly glowy mood—gifted, like curses were things that simply didn't exist, but never, never cursed.

But maybe there was not more truth to that than any of the other rumors surrounding the girls. What's known—what can be agreed upon—is this: the girls were different. Cursed or gifted, it's all just hearsay.

There were other whispers—crueler ones, maybe—that it wasn't a curse at all but a penance, a punishment brought down from on high to bear out on the girls for the sins of their parents. Their father was a drunk and God only knew what their mother's shortcomings might've been, aside from leaving them, of course.

Before things had gone bad, though, when their father still had more good days than bad and their mother hadn't up and left yet, their mother insisted it was a gift.

And Lena couldn't lie, but even she knew that couldn't possibly be the truth.

. . .

Isa was swinging idly on the swing set off to the side of the schoolyard, reading a book she'd borrowed from what passed for a lending library in town, waiting for Lena to get done with classes. She'd skipped out early again today, though despite an occasional slap on the wrist or threat of detention, nobody ever did much about it.

Nobody ever did much at all about Isa, really. It wasn't so much that they didn't know what to do with her, as they didn't care to figure out anything to do with her—and without a doubt what they already knew didn't work.

It would've taken time to meet her halfway or try to understand her, and that was time they'd rather spend somewhere else, doing just about anything else. Isa was difficult and unruly and almost impossible to understand, and that make her more work than she was worth.

And that's the way of things when you're different, isn't it?

Lipreading was difficult and ineffective—not that hearing people ever cared to know—especially if you weren't allowed to sit to the front of class, because your eyesight was perfectly fine, Isa, save those spots for the nearsighted kids and just follow along in the book.

The slapdash mix of what little ASL she'd picked up (back when the school could still afford the assistant they'd brought in for her) and the homesign she'd made up herself with her sister and mother, that worked well enough. And so what did she care? If they wouldn't bother to teach her, or even try to understand her, why should she care to meet them at whatever arbitrary halfway point they dictated?

Books, at least, never pretended to be anything other than what they were.

So she skipped out early again today, and other than a few frustrated glances and age-old renditions of you'll never learn anything if you don't try, she was left alone to it. As long as they didn't say anything to her daddy she didn't much care either way. Not that he'd mind—she'd heard him say on more than one occasion that school wasn't of any use for his girls, they'd already learned all they needed to know by fifth grade, just like him.

Then again, maybe he would mind. Who could tell when or what might set him off into a fury? And though Isa wasn't scared of him exactly, not for herself—Lena, not gifted the excuse of silence, often took the brunt of his moods—it would be plenty foolish to push his limits.

Isa scoured out a line in the dirt beneath the swing set with the toe of her boot, digging deeper as she moved back and forth.

Last bell had rung half an hour ago, and by the time Lena got done tutoring younger kids or whatever it was she was doing, they were running late. Isa skipped down the sidewalk next to her sister, who kept trying to hurry her along as she played a game of haltingly skipping over cracks in the sidewalk on their way into town.

Step on a crack, break your mama's back; step on a line, break your daddy's spine.

Isa, hurry up, Lena signed at her, pulling at her wrist to try to make her move faster.

No stepping on cracks, Isa reminded her, but Lena said she was too old for that.

Step on a crack, break your mama's back; step on a line, break your daddy's spine. Well, Isa's mama was long gone and her daddy might not even care that much so long as he got some good painkillers out of it.

That's not real, don't be silly. Lena didn't sign, she snapped—Isa could tell from the sharp movement of her jaw. *I'm too old for that; we both are.*

She scuffed her feet, but stopped skipping, following her sister as she guided her bike into town. Of course it wasn't real, that wasn't the point—Lena always understood that before.

. . .

They stopped in at the store on the way home. Denny, the boy from school that everybody knew Isa liked, or had, until she caught him making fun of the way she never talked, was working the counter.

Lena went up to talk to him while Isa grabbed what they needed.

Hey Denny, said Lena.

Hey, he said, glancing up from the magazine he was reading. His eyes flickered between her and Isa, grabbing items off the shelves behind her, suspiciously. *Y'all need any help?*

Whatever she gets, plus two bags of hog feed, Lena told him, without batting an eye. *Biggest ones you've got.*

Denny grunted his response, going out back to grab the bags of hog feed from the storeroom.

Lena hummed and turned around. Everyone knew what the hog feed was for—wasn't like it was a secret. Half the town, at least, got their liquor from the Larkins and the other half quietly held their tongues, judging and clutching at Bibles from afar.

It wasn't like there was any police force to speak of in these parts, and anyway, so long as nobody got too sick, they wouldn't bother with some backyard bootlegger plying his trade. Especially one as mean as Billy Larkin.

Denny came out, dragging two great big bags of hog feed behind him, and Isa joined them up at the counter. She plopped down two cokes, a package of cookies, a pound of sugar, a jar of honey, and twelve sticks of the beef jerky their daddy liked to chew on while he worked.

Isa hip-checked Lena as they waited for Denny to count everything up. He didn't say anything to her, and she was giving him a steely look that plainly said he had better not, anyway. At least he was being nice enough to Lena which counted as more than something in Isa's book.

Isa didn't have friends because she didn't want to have anything to do with them (and good enough, because they didn't want anything to do with her either), but Lena had had friends once. Having friends and losing them was worse than never having them at all—or at least is seemed that way to Isa who didn't have any lost friends to compare it to.

Denny must've felt the discomfort of being the one silently judged for once—and good, thought Isa, let him—because he tried to fill the silence with small talk.

Y'all hear there's a new doctor in town? he asked, conversational as he rang them up.

New doctor?

Sure, said Denny, *just down the street.*

Isa signed something and then rolled her eyes, but Denny was watching Lena. *You met 'em?*

Nah. Heard he's from the city, though.

That was code for not from around here which was code for outsider which was code for not to be trusted until proved trustworthy.

Fella named Pacey. Something Pacey.

Huh, said Lena.

Yeah, said Denny.

Anyway, thanks, said Lena, handing over a collection of bills and holding out her hand for change. Gossip was gossip, but that didn't mean they had to hang around.

Mmm-hmmm, said Denny, already focused back on his magazine as they scooped up their stuff and left.

. . .

A new doctor, Lena said, sounding almost dreamy as they started off toward the bike they'd left leaning up against the storefront. *He could know something—something the old doctor didn't.*

She said it like it was something Isa might not realize on her own, like it was an original-Lena-thought, and that was what soured Isa to the possibility she knew her sister was getting at.

Plenty of people thought Isa was simple, because she couldn't hear or talk and didn't ever do much in school, because they couldn't understand her, maybe. Lena was her only mouthpiece to the rest of the world, and sometimes Isa resented her for that—especially when her sister got dreamy and forgot she wasn't simple, just like the rest of them.

So what, she signed, *and maybe he doesn't.*

Lena wasn't watching her though; she was too busy thinking about a future where she didn't have to only tell the truth, didn't have to only be her sister's voice. A future where they were free.

. . .

The woodsy, smoky musk of their holler was something comfortingly familiar, something banal in way that only home can be. But certain scents still stood out, and sometimes, Lena could swear she still smelled their mother. She was eight-years gone and nothing but a memory, but, sometimes, Lena could swear she still smelled the honeysuckle sweet scent of her hands after she'd been out working in the yard, the buttery-flour smell after she'd been baking and would wipe white streaks of dust across her apron, the sharp, astringent burning of fresh moonshine as they helped her can and sort the newest batch.

That last one was still commonplace around the Larkin house, of course, nothing unusual about that. Home always smelled at least a little of moonshine and honey.

But the others? The others Lena couldn't explain.

Daddy and Isa never mentioned it—even when the smell was so strong and sweet she could almost gag over it—so she never did say anything about it.

After all, a secret wasn't the same as a lie. Lena had to tell the truth, but that didn't mean she had to tell everything.

▪ ▪ ▪

Daddy was leaning next to the open window of a green pickup when they got home.

Isa hopped off the handlebars, hitched her backpack over her shoulders, and ran off toward the house while Lena was still backpedaling to slow her descent across the gravel driveway, kicking up a trail of dust.

Lena swung wide around the pickup but threw up a silent wave as she passed them by, not wanting to interrupt business talk. See, they sold a lot of their stock through word of mouth and house visits, but the rest went out farther afield, and it was the Hartfords who helped with that.

Jake Hartford and his sister Doe were grown—several years out of school, anyway—and they ran the product out through town and farther still. Lena didn't like them much, but that was personal and didn't have anything to do with business, which they did just fine as far as she knew.

She leaned her bike up against the porch and leaned down to scratch behind the tomcat's scruffy neck (the one she was pretty sure Isa had named Earl for some reason). It squirmed out of her reach and slipped through the latticework under the porch. Crossing her arms, she turned back and watched daddy as he finished up with the Hartfords. He slapped a hand against the roof of the truck and waved them on their way.

Not wanting to be caught standing around, Lena joined her sister inside.

Over supper that night, the girls were sitting across from their daddy and cleaning out unblessed bowls full of chili and a cast iron skillet of cornbread. He was digging into his bowl, sopping up chili with a sponge of cornbread and shoveling it down with unrestrained gusto. They went through their usual ritual where he asked about school, and Lena pretended it had been fine, and he pretended to be interested.

Then daddy fixed his gaze on Isa, narrowing his eyes like a hunter looking down the scope. *You lay out of school again?* he asked her. He didn't sign; he never did.

She pursed her lips up real tight.

Don't you lie to me now, girl.

Lena watched Isa examine his expression with a calculating look, then her mouth spread into a smile and she nodded.

Lena held her breath, waiting for the reaction, but daddy just laughed.

No question you're mine, he said.

Isa smirked and gave Lena a look that said, *told you so,* without saying anything at all.

How Isa, who skipped class and disobeyed the rules and surely would've talked back if she could've, still managed to be the golden child, was anyone's guess—and Lena couldn't've said if she was grateful or resentful of that fact. Maybe a bit of both.

They lapsed into silence over their bowls of chili after

that and, continuing their act of pretending, pretended it wasn't as stilted and uncomfortable as it was.

To fill the silence—because Lena, always the one to fill them, found them especially uncomfortable—she mentioned she'd heard tell of this new doctor in town. Daddy grunted in acknowledgement.

Isa signed something and Lena gave her a sharp look before turning back to her bowl and saying casually as she could, *I was thinking maybe we might could go see him after school tomorrow.*

That had him looking up. *What for?* he asked.

Lena shrugged, chancing a furtive glance over at her sister who was avoiding her gaze in very un-Isa-like fashion. She contrived to shrug. (Those kind of lies, she had found, didn't really count as lies, and that was handy.)

Oh, you know, nothing really. Just to see what's what—heard he's from the city and all, said Lena

Daddy scoffed. *Big city man,* he said like it might've just as well been a curse. He took another big bit of chili, some of the juice dripping down his chin before he wiped it away with a harsh swipe of his napkin. *What you know about him anyway, huh?*

Not much, said Lena. *Just what Denny—you know, from the store—just what he could tell us. Name's Pacey, I think.*

His head shot up so suddenly, Lena flinched back against her seat. The mood, which had been of a normal, casual disinterest, turned just as suddenly sour. The sisters shared a look, not sure what to make of it, and equally sure it wouldn't end well for either of them.

Daddy's ill moods always boded ill for them as well.

What'd you say? he asked, focus turned entirely from his bowl to his eldest daughter.

Sir? she asked, because she wasn't entirely sure what he was getting at and better to make a non-answer than to say something wrong.

I said, daddy said, like he would only repeat himself this once and she had better not ask again, *what did you just say?*

Lena swallowed. *I said—about the new doctor—Denny told me his name's Pacey or something, sir, and he's new in town.*

Their daddy let out a hiss like a snake, pissed and ready to strike. But instead of doing anything, he glared into his bowl of chili, his forehead creased into three, deep lines. Lena and Isa cautiously went back to eating in silence, trying not to break this tentative peace, whatever it might mean.

It wasn't until they were finished drying the bowls and spoons he handed to them as he finished washing, and Lena was moving toward the back bedroom where she and Isa slept, that he grabbed her by the arm to stop her. His fingers dug into the flesh of her arm, not quite painful, but only just.

Isa froze by the door, tense, waiting to see what would happen.

That doctor, he said, his eyes locking on hers, *you're not to go see him, you understand?*

Lena nodded quickly—maybe too quickly. His grip tightened.

Yessir, said Lena, praying this could be the end of it.

I want to hear you say it, he said, flat and dangerous.

Okay, she said.

He slammed the flat of his palm against the counter. Lena jolted and Isa's eyes squinted against a glare that would get her in too much trouble if he saw it.

I understand, said Lena. *We won't go to the doctor.*

The words were like cotton stuffing pulled from her throat. They weren't a lie, they weren't a lie, they weren't a lie—but the pounding in her head told her even she knew that wasn't entirely true.

Lena grabbed Isa's hand and they scurried back to the bedroom just slow enough to keep from catching his notice any further, but he was too busy grabbing a bottle of moonshine from the cabinet and chugging it in a series of jagged gulps before slamming that down on the counter, too.

. . .

For all their mama's insistence that everything about her girls was a gift, their daddy told a different story. His went like this:

Way back when, before Lena was even a worry in his mind, he brewed up a fresh batch of moonshine, sold it to a man passing through, some city-slicker never tasted liquor that strong in his life. Something'd gone wrong, though, and the batch was bad—daddy never said how. Anyway, the man went blind and must've had some kind of dark magic about him, because not nine months later Lena was born and Isa not long after. The curse was a curse, and according to daddy it was of his own making.

And everybody knew the rest.

. . .

Lena dragged Isa out of bed early the next morning.

Where we going? Isa signed.

Lena didn't answer.

Isa was still rubbing the sleep from her eyes as Lena was pushing her up to perch on the handlebars of their bike and pedaling hard and fast into town. She hadn't even changed out of her gingham pajama pants, just thrown a sweatshirt on over them.

Lena pedaled hard and fast into town. It was a Saturday, meaning things were a little less tired than usual, and they passed several people they knew on the street.

How y'all girls doing? Mrs. Manor asked as they rode by. Isa waved at her.

Mr. Jacobson stopped them on the sidewalk where Lena had locked her bike up to a streetlamp. *Hey girls, how's that daddy of yours? Wouldn't happen to have a new batch of honey ready, would he?* he asked, throwing the pleasantries out quick before getting to the real concern.

Honey was what most people called their daddy's special brew of moonshine, because he made it with honey and it was fresh and sweet—or, at least, that's what everybody said.

He's just fine, Mr. Jacobson, and we've got a new batch ready at the house, said Lena. *You can stop by later if you want.*

He nodded. *I might just do that.*

Lena smiled, big and bright, until he walked off.

Isa, who had been standing next to her sister this whole time, pressed a fist against her eyes, finally half-awake. She grabbed at Lena's wrist to get her attention. *What are we doing out here?* she signed.

Lena pulled a couple of books out of the canvas bag slung over her shoulder in answer. *Gotta return these books to the library,* she said.

Isa frowned. They were her books, and she knew they

weren't due—and due was a loose term here anyway, since the library wasn't so much a library as a shelf in the corner of the store where people left a book or took a book—for at least another week or so. She wasn't sure exactly what Lena was getting at here, but she was pretty sure she was about to get dragged into it whatever it was.

She didn't fight her on it, though, and just followed her as she went into the store, the little bells above the door jingling, and returned the books, letting Isa pick out a few more. They paid for a couple of cokes on the way out and sipped them as Lena led them further into town.

By the time they passed the butcher, Isa understood what was happening. Just down the street, across from the post office, was a building with a sign on the windows for the new doctor. Joel Pacey, M.D., it said in white print on the glass.

Isa sighed, glanced at her sister, and took off across the street. Lena said, *wait, stop,* as she chased after Isa, because she had to for this to work. *We told daddy—*

But Isa ignored her, pushing through the door. It wasn't that she resented Lena using her this way, exactly—they both did what they had to do to get by—it was that Isa wished Lena could just let it go, sometimes.

(Maybe it was that Isa was pretty sure the reason Lena wanted to break the curse so bad had more to do with her resenting Isa than wanting to be able to lie—after all, she'd gotten pretty good at manipulating the truth to her own ends, anyway.

Just look where they were now.)

There was a line of chairs in front of the glass-front windows and a counter beside a door leading to a back room, but nobody behind it. Isa shuffled awkwardly, but Lena moved forward, calling out a tentative, *hello?*

A man showing the first hints of gray with gentle lines framing his eyes walked out to greet them. He was wearing a plaid shirt and no white lab coat, though a stethoscope hung loose around his neck. *Can I help you?* he asked, squinting down at them.

Lena nodded, *yes please.*

He gave her a bemused look, clearly expecting more of an explanation than that, and Isa sighed in exasperation. For someone perfectly able to talk to anyone, sometimes Lena could hardly manage even the simplest exchange.

Tell him we need a checkup, Isa signed at her sister.

The doctor was watching her with interest as Lena turned back to him and said, *A checkup?*

Sure, right through here. He waved them into the back room, which was hardly bigger than a supply closet and had only an exam table, a chair, and a counter covered in medical supplies.

Isa hopped up on the exam table and Lena stood next to her. Seemingly finding her courage again, Lena said, *we need your help,* before the doctor had even finished washing up his hands.

He turned around, and looked both of them over with careful eyes. *Alright. What kind of help?*

His voice was soft and soothing and somehow familiar, though Isa couldn't say why. He reminded her vaguely of the nice doctors she sometimes saw on TV.

You're new to town, said Lena, which of course was true, and the doctor laughed a little, if awkwardly. Maybe this wasn't the first time he'd heard it.

Yes, he said, tugging at the stethoscope so that it listed to one side.

So, you don't know, of course, said Lena. Then, as simple as could be, *we're cursed.*

The doctor blinked, face going suddenly, carefully blank. *I'm sorry?* he asked.

We're cursed, Lena said again.

I don't understand, said the doctor.

I can't lie, Lena said, *and my sister, she can't speak—or hear, but that's not the real problem.*

Oh? said the doctor, glancing at Isa and back at Lena and then, *oh.*

He turned around and began washing his hands again. Isa wasn't sure this was a particularly good sign, but she glanced at her sister for confirmation that the conversation was going as badly as she thought. It was always possible she'd misread the doctor's lips somewhere, but Lena's frown lines told a different story.

Dr. Pacey—Lena began.

What are your names? the doctor asked, turning back to them as he dried off his hands with a paper towel.

Um, Lena, said Lena, and Isa signed her name, which Lena quickly translated as being Isa for the doctor's benefit.

The doctor nodded as if this was what he'd feared, the lines around his eyes deepening in thought. *You're Billy Larkin's girls,* he said—not a question.

Isa nodded.

He sighed even more deeply, leaning back against the counter and looking away from them. Isa watched the shape of his lips carefully as he said, *I'm not sure you should be here.*

Isa had expected a lot of things, but she hadn't expected that.

What? Lena exclaimed so loudly, Isa could hear the outline of it in her better ear.

I just—I don't think it's a good idea for you girls to be here.

Your father—

Our father doesn't own us, Lena said angrily.

The doctor nodded. *I know that. But I don't think he'd like it, you being here. Am I wrong?*

What do you care? Lena said. *You're a doctor. It's your job to help us.*

Isa reached a hand out to touch her sister's shoulder, just barely making contact because she could tell Lena was about to shake right out of her own skin, wound up as she was.

The doctor pressed a hand to his forehead, like he was smoothing away stray thoughts. He nodded. *Okay. You're right,* he said. Then, *A cure?*

Lena nodded, and Isa nodded with her but it was mostly for solidarity's sake—it had always been more Lena's curse than hers. She'd never felt any ownership over it the way her sister had, never stayed up nights worrying about it or dreamed of a different future. Life was here and the curse was here and that was how things were.

Things weren't so bad, anyhow.

Isa looked up in time to catch the latter half of whatever the doctor had been saying to Lena, trying to shape the movements of his lips into words.

There are some options, of course. Cochlear implants, speech therapy, but those all work best on young children, you understand.

The doctor spoke slowly and clearly, and Lena translated the words Isa couldn't make out for herself—though most of them were still too unfamiliar to make any sense.

Lena nodded slowly, but Isa couldn't help noticing the only cures she mentioned were for her, not Lena.

And Lena? Isa signed when it became clear her sister wasn't asking.

Lena glanced at her, swallowed, and then asked, as if scared of the answer even more than the lack of one, *What about me?*

The doctor sighed. Another question he didn't want to answer, another answer he didn't want to give. Isa glanced at her sister and braced for the fallout.

Is it possible—have you considered, the doctor began gently, *that this isn't a curse at all?*

Of course it's a curse, snapped Lena. *What else would it be?*

Life? The way things are?

Isa winced. Too indelicate, too blunt (too honest). She could see the building pressure of keeping her emotions contained puffing out her sisters cheeks, waited for the explosion.

No. Lena shook her head. *I don't believe that.*

It's okay to be different—there's nothing wrong with it, the doctor said, a careful diagnosis. *I know you girls must not have many resources here, but maybe—*

You can't help; you could've just said.

And, then, instead of exploding, Isa watched her sister deflate.

Come on, Isa, Lena signed, helping her down from the exam table so she wouldn't have to look at the furrowed face of the doctor.

He followed them into the waiting room. *I'm sorry, I know this can't be easy—*

What do you know? Lena said, and Isa could see that her sister was on the verge of tears so she grabbed her hand and shot a sharp glare at the doctor as Lena swung the door open and marched them outside. *You don't know anything.*

The last thing Isa saw before the door swung shut behind them was the doctor, watching them leave with a look of fathomless regret.

■ ■ ■

Lena knew disappointment and rejection all too well. She was the girl who'd outed herself without much choice in the matter the first time she'd played truth or dare in grade school. Some kid had asked her about her crush. Everyone expected Tommy Yeats, the boy who'd tried to kiss her out in the schoolyard, but when she said Patience Early, instead, that was pretty much the end of that.

Being cursed was easier to forgive, apparently.

Lying wasn't just a way to get away with things you oughtn't to get away with—like moonshining or disobeying rules, like daddy thought; sometimes, it was a way to survive. Lying was choice, and you should get a choice—what you choose to tell, who you choose to tell it to.

So Lena knew disappointment, and she knew curses, and she knew how to bottle it up real tight until you could pretend it didn't hurt anymore. She was good at that.

■ ■ ■

They didn't talk about what happened with the doctor that night, not when they got home to find the house empty, and certainly not when daddy came to get them to help him with a new batch of moonshine. He had the mash they'd mixed up last night cooking out on the furnace in the woods.

Give that a good stir for me there, Lena, he said as he enlisted Isa's help to dump the pot with the rest of the mash mix into the huge still.

The mash was thick and viscous in the copper pot, and Lena had to fight against it to make careful rotations with the long spoon she was using to stir. The third stir churned up an unfortunate thing—a chipmunk carcass, drowned or boiled, whichever got him first.

Eugh, said Lena, stepping quickly away from the pot. Daddy looked over with a frown to see what caused the commotion.

Ah, he said when he saw the furry little body floating on top of his corn mash. He glanced at Lena, before turning to Isa instead. *Fish that outta there for me, Isa, that a girl.*

Isa grabbed the handle of the spoon from her sister and used it to fish out the dead chipmunk and toss it off into the woods. She took over stirring.

Daddy glanced down into the mash mixture with a considered eye. *Eh, that'll be fine,* he said and poured in an extra-large helping of sugar and honey to mask whatever lingered.

▪ ▪ ▪

Isa was drawing honeybees on a stack of thin, metal mason jar lids they'd use to can up the newest batch of moonshine as soon as it was cooked when her sister burst into the room to tell her she had a new plan. For what, Isa wasn't sure. She glanced at the small pile of finished lids and the stack leaning ominously beside it that had yet to be done and decided that whatever Lena had in mind was better than that.

(She was wrong, of course, but only time would tell that.)

Lena had the recipe pulled up on the computer, the old desktop their parents got back before the girls were even born, and Isa squinted down at the screen.

Casts and Curses:
What They Are and How to Break Them

There was more text underneath that, but Isa skimmed down to the part her sister highlighted with the blinking cursor:

> Breaking A Blood Curse.
>
> Blood curses—of any nonspecific variety—are inherited or lifelong curses present in the cursed since birth, or even before. They can range widely in outcome and severity, but are always harmful in nature and thus require special care in breaking. This recipe should help with any common blood curses. For more advanced curses, please see Cursed Objects, Sleeping Curses, or Wasting Curses.
>
> What you'll need:
>
> ▪ a binding agent (syrup, honey, or even nontoxic glue will do in a pinch)
> ▪ a houseplant (preferably one the cursed has spent time around)

- three drops (each) of the cursed's blood

The rest read like a recipe: flour, baking soda, cloves, two tablespoons of fresh lemon juice, and a portion of your last meal—thought that last one struck Isa as odd.

> Step 1. Allow the houseplant to mature under a full moon.
>
> Step 2. Mix together the binding agent, flour, baking soda, cloves, lemon juice, and last meal. Boil down to liquid. Let cool.
>
> Step 3. Stir three time clockwise. Add fully matured houseplant. Stir three times counterclockwise.
>
> Step 4. Allow to cook for five minutes at a simmer.
>
> Step 5. Add blood—freshly spilled—and meditate on the source of the curse and the desired outcome for at least three minutes.
>
> *** Note: please follow these instructions carefully. *Casts and Curses* bears no responsibility for wrongly brewed potions.

Isa frowned at the screen. *What is this?* she signed,

even though she knew exactly what it was.

Lena gave her a long look. *A cure,* she said. And the *obviously* wasn't said, but it was heavily implied. *The doctor couldn't help, so we're gonna do it the old fashioned way.*

And in a weird way, that made sense to Isa, so even though she thought this whole thing was kind of ridiculous, she agreed to help.

They had to improvise a little—after all, the full moon wasn't for another week, and they didn't have time to wait according to Lena, and the only houseplant around was the old aloe plant they used for burns, but since it was all they had, Lena said it would have to do.

Lena grabbed honey, flour, baking soda, and a whole lemon from the cabinet and then, after considering, took the pepper too, because that was as close to cloves as they had in the house. Isa grabbed the aloe plant off the counter and tucked it under her arm, pot and all, as she followed Lena to the still in the backyard.

The still was empty, waiting for the next batch of moonshine they were supposed to start mixing up tonight. They'd have to be quick about it—the still had to be cleared out and cleaned before daddy got back from town—so Lena turned up the heat and started adding ingredients, letting the mixture rise to a boil.

The last meal either of them had eaten was a bowl of honey nut cheerios with 2% milk, so Isa ran back to grab the box and they poured out the rest of that and several splashes of milk to the mixture, wrinkling their noises as the worsening smell.

It was starting to turn a foul midnight green color and the fumes were strong and singed the hairs in Isa's nose.

Is it supposed to look like that? Isa signed, uncertainly.

Lena just frowned, and Isa knew that meant she wasn't

sure either.

Lena tossed the lemon in whole and said, *we still have to add the aloe. And blood. Besides, potions aren't meant to be pleasant, right? Otherwise anyone would use them.*

Isa wasn't so sure, but she waited for Lena to stir three times clockwise before pulling the aloe from its plastic pot and tossing it in. Lena stirred counterclockwise. They counted out five minutes, and when they were up Lena pulled out a small sewing needle she'd swiped from their mother's old mending kit.

Ready? she asked.

Isa nodded, even though she wasn't really sure she was, and her sister carefully pricked her finger with the needle, pinching the tip until three drops of blood rippled into the surface of the mixture. She repeated the process on herself, and then they both stared down into the pot with anxious eyes.

The mixture had turned tar black and thick in the pot, and the surface bubbled sluggishly. The fumes were almost noxious, and when Lena pulled out a spoonful for closer inspection, Isa stumbled back and Lena raised a sleeve to cover her mouth and nose as she choked over the smell.

We can't drink that, Isa signed, *It's poison.*

It's not poison, said Lena, but it lacked any real strength, and Isa was almost surprised she was able to get the words past her lips, lie that they were.

Lena glared down at it, but she didn't move to take a sip. It wasn't anything like how castsandcurses.com had suggested it should turn out. It probably really was as likely to kill them as cure them.

Before Lena could do anything, though, it started to corrode the metal of the spoon, and Isa knocked it out of her hand.

We have to get rid of it, Isa signed with a worried glance at the simmering tar in the pot. It was starting to stick and burn against the copper sides of the still, and it was sure to be a chore to clean out, if the still wasn't ruined for good.

Isa moved to grab one side of the still and dump it, but Lena grabbed her. *No!* she gasped, not ready to let it go.

Isa turned, brows drawn down.

We might still be able to fix it, Lena said weakly.

But Isa shook her head, unwilling to play along like this with their lives—and certainly their stomachs—at stake.

Don't you want a cure? Lena asked—signed, for Isa's benefit. *Don't you want to talk again?*

Isa clicked her teeth together in a harsh snap she could feel vibrate through the bones in her jaw. *I can talk,* she signed.

You know that's not what I mean, Lena said, looking halfway to ashamed.

But Isa was tired and more than that Isa was done pretending, pretending she believed this, pretending she didn't understand why her sister wanted this, pretending they both didn't resent each other for it.

That's not what you really care about, though, is it? Isa signed.

I don't have to tell you that, said Lena, but she blushed red.

Isa wrinkled her nose in disdain. *Drink it then,* she signed. She started to storm off, but Lena grabbed her wrist again, more gently this time.

No, I'm sorry, you're right. It's not worth it, she signed. *Help me clean it up?*

And she did, scouring the still clean with her sister's help. But when Isa wasn't looking, Lena scraped a small bit off. She saved it in a bottle, tucking it away in her back pocket under the long, flannel tail of her shirt.

A few dark drops had landed on her hand, though. She wiped them away quickly, before Isa could see, but they left stinging, raw spots on her skin. She pulled her sleeves over her hands, feeling childish and a little heartbroken.

They walked back to the house, backs turned to the forest where all around the still, the brush withered brown and died.

. . .

The helicopter-blade seeds of the sugar maples spun through the air on a shift of wind. They drifted all around Lena as she checked that Isa and daddy weren't around before pulling up a piece of loose siding that had rotted off the wall. It was her little hidey-hole. Her secret place.

Inside it was the bottled potion she'd carefully stored away.

She reached in to grab it, but the glass neck of the old coke bottle broke off in her hand, shattering against the ground and slashing potion up onto her fingers and wrist. She gasped and wiped it off on the grass.

Her hand was raw to the touch, but Lena was more concerned with all the dreams of a cure shattered and melting into the ground at her feet.

She let out a frustrated growl and aimed a kick at the wall that knocked off another piece of siding, then, suddenly spent, collapsed back against the house.

Why did it matter so much to her anyway? Deception could offer protection, sure, and Lena knew the curse had robbed her of an armor of lies, but so what? Would breaking the curse really change anything, here?

No. That was the truth, and Lena knew it with sudden clarity. A cure wouldn't change a thing, not really.

Maybe that was what Isa had always known—why she only ever went along with Lena's schemes, never really put any heart into them like she'd wanted.

Maybe daddy was right, and if they tended to the still long enough, well enough, they'd break the curse just like that—but Lena had never really believed that lie, anyway.

She wanted to believe there was a simple answer to everything—the shortest line from point A to B—but those answers weren't always so agreeable, either. Like the doctor who told her that honeysuckle scent she smelled something wasn't anything special, just a sensory hallucination, a medical condition they could treat just like so if only she'd let them.

She didn't.

So what did it matter if the truth wasn't any better than the lies people told themselves?

(Except she never had a choice—and didn't that make all the difference?)

When Isa asked her later, Lena was still too raw to reveal any of this to her little sister. Instead she said, *leave me alone,* and Isa did.

▪ ▪ ▪

Isa was reaching through the wooden lattice underneath the front porch, trying to snag the scruff of one of the kittens that had gotten away from its mama. Lena was sitting on the steps, picking at the frayed laces of her boots. They both pretended not to notice the other.

Isa'd been ignoring her sister since their fight yesterday and was perfectly content to keep on like that, but the electricity went out, and since daddy had gone off to make some money to pay it off, it likely wouldn't be back for some time, which meant they were both stuck outside, at least until dark.

Something swiped at her and Isa withdrew, sucking at the small droplets of blood dewing across the scratches on the back of her hand.

Let me see, Lena said, sounding annoyed.

It's fine, Isa signed, left-handed and short since her right was still stinging sore.

Lena ignored her, getting up and moving to check the scratches. *Go wash so you don't get cat-scratch fever or something.*

But Lena hissed when the movement jostled her arm, and Isa frowned at her. The edges of her sleeve were pulled long over her fist so Isa couldn't see her hand at all. Suspicious.

Let me see, Isa signed and grabbed at Lena's arm.

Lena screamed, a piercing terrible thing that would ring in Isa's ears for years to come. She scrambled back, but not before Isa managed to push up her sleeve. An awful, blackish rot was spreading up her arm, eating the flesh and drying the life right out of her. Isa understood immediately what it was.

You drank it? she signed, but Lena's eyes were closed in pain, so Isa tugged at her shirt insistently until she opened her eyes to see what she was saying.

No, no, Lena managed, closing her eyes again. *Spilled.*

She clutched the blackening arm against her chest, moaning as she leaned back against the railing of the porch to keep from falling over.

Isa could see it, clear as day: her sister, standing right in front of her, dying. The rot was killing her, from the tips of her fingers up through her arm.

I'm sorry, Lena gritted between her teeth, and then signed just to make sure her sister understood it. *I'm sorry.*

The blacked rot was twisting up her arm in long, creeping tendrils, and Lena slid down against the front of the porch, legs giving out underneath her.

Isa didn't know what to do. She thought Lena might've whispered something like, *it's okay,* but it wasn't, it wasn't. She was dying, and that was supposed to just be okay? Whatever Lena might think, Isa knew otherwise.

She couldn't let her sister die. Wouldn't. Maybe that was selfish—to want that more than anything, more than Lena's happiness or safety. More than Lena's own wishes, even. Isa couldn't let her sister die, that was what she knew, so she did the only thing she could think to do: she ran into the house, past the doorway and the shotgun lying on the mantle, past the table and the cold fireplace, grabbed the great, big hunting knife their mother used to use for skinning and cleaning the wild game daddy drug home.

She ran back outside and found her sister lying on the ground, eyes closed, breathing shallow.

Isa's own breath hitched in her chest, coming out in a wheeze. She tugged Lena's oversized flannel off over her shoulders, revealing the left arm blackened up almost to the elbow. Isa wheezed again—quick and sharp to get through the bone, just like daddy beheading the copperhead. She steadied her grip on the knife with both hands.

No second thoughts. She brought the knife down, cleaving the rotted black clear from the flesh. Lena's screams peaked and then whimpered out as she fainted. The withered arm that used to belong to her sister jerked against the ground. The fingers seemed to claw at the earth, alive all on its own, and Isa gave it a good thunk with the flat side of the knife that stopped it moving.

Lena wasn't moving, either. Her eyelids closed and so paper thin Isa could trace a checker pattern of purple veins across them. She didn't want to think about that, so instead she grabbed the flannel shirt she'd tossed aside and wrapped it around the bleeding stump of her sister's arm as tight as she could, but the blood soaked through, turning the dirt around them to mud and staining Isa's fingers red.

A whimper scraped out of her throat, and Isa swiped at her damp cheeks as she searched furiously for something to stop the bleeding.

But the blood just wouldn't stop. It was everywhere—on Lena, on Isa, on their clothes and the ground and even the kitten mewling beside the porch for its mama. Everywhere but where it was supposed to be, inside Lena.

She had cut off her sister's arm. She had cut off her sister's arm, but she was still dying—except now, if she died, it would be all Isa's fault.

She had to set that aside, push it down. Isa scrubbed at her eyes with the edge of her bloody sleeve—but she couldn't think about that either. She needed to focus, and she needed to get help, but first she had to at least slow the bleeding or Lena would die right here.

Right. A tourniquet. She ran inside and grabbed one of her father's old belts, tightening it as best she could around Lena's arm. She marked the spot, then slipped it off and cut a hole in the leather a few inches past that. She took a deep breath to steady the shaking in her hands.

Lena woke again, howling, as Isa pulled the belt tight and then even tighter around her arm, wrapping it all up again once she was sure the bleeding had slowed.

Isa wiped at the sweaty hair sticking to her forehead, smearing blood all across her face. Lena whimpered quietly.

Her eyes were barely open, but that didn't stop Isa from signing over and over again, with fingers that had gone entirely numb:

I'm sorry I'm sorry I'm sorry I'm sorry I'm sorry

▪ ▪ ▪

Lena's opened her eyes to a blurry, throbbing world, trees and a blue sky overhead and her little sister crying and crying and signing something frantically—Lena couldn't tell what.

She blinked, trying to focus, but her head was stuffed full of cloth, heavy and slow. She tried to speak, to ask, *what,* but nothing came out—she couldn't tell if her lips even moved at all. Her arm, where the unbearable pain had been burning her alive before, throbbed in time with her heartbeat, but was otherwise suspiciously painless.

Lena tried to sit up to look down at it, but all she saw was her sister standing over her, a bloody knife still clutched knuckle-white in her hand.

▪ ▪ ▪

It's okay, said Lena. *I'm okay.*

And, *It's not your fault.*

And, *I'm safe. We're safe. It's okay.*

And Isa knew her sister could never lie, so it would've

been easy to believe her.

. . .

Later, Isa wouldn't be sure how she managed to bundle Lena up and prop her on the handlebars of their bike to ride into town, but somehow she did.

The doctor, when they walked into his office, blood-soaked, Lena's right arm wrapped around Isa's neck to keep upright, was frantic.

How did this happen? he cried, helping Lena into the backroom.

His eyes caught on the flannel shirt wrapped around Lena's stump, the blood splatter coating Isa's arms and shirt and face, eyed them like something straight out of a horror film. Something in the stiff remove of his posture spoke to a mistrust, a wariness, something just as deep—and maybe even more raw—than all the townspeople who whispered how that doctor *wasn't from around here.* The lift of his shoulders looked ready to take flight. He was considering what events brought the girls to his office, bloodied and blanched, and, Isa thought, maybe weighing the relative consequences of calling for the sheriff—far out of town as he might be.

Accident, Lena bit out finally, and Isa was surprised, not because it was a lie, exactly—her sister had become adept at half-truths and convincing herself of whatever she wanted to be true—but because it implied that not only wasn't it Lena's fault, it wasn't Isa's either.

It calmed the doctor into an uneasy peace, though. Long enough for him to tend to Lena's arm, anyway. Cleaned her, stitched her, drugged her, made her ragdoll whole.

Her head lolled as the doctor filled her up with fresh blood from a bag, eyes glassy distant in a way Isa feared almost as much as she had feared the spreading rot. She had seen the way drugs could spread through a body, made them boneless and content to be, but the doctor said she was going into shock and they should really take her to the hospital and *please, Isa, let go of my arm and let me help your sister,* so she did.

Isa felt numb and sightless, too, but the doctor didn't give her anything for it. She looked down to check that her arms were still there, and they were but she couldn't feel them all the same. Ghost limbs, haunted and haunting her for what she'd done.

The doctor said something, and she wasn't looking, but when he tapped her shoulder to get her attention she jerked back reproachfully.

Sorry, she saw him mouth. *Sorry.* She nodded.

Are you hurt? She shook her head. No.

He was unconvinced, but she still held herself away from him, distrusting him for no reason aside from the fact that he was here and he was helping and he was seeing them like this.

How did all this happen? he asked again, now that Lena was stable enough and there was time for questions again.

Accident, Isa signed and mouthed at the same time. It felt like scratchy wool against her lips. She glanced at where the doctor had laid Lena with a blanket pillowed under her head, skin ashen pale.

And your father—where was he when all this, he motioned vaguely toward Lena, *happened?*

Isa frowned, shook her head. She gestured off toward the middle distance, indicating *off, out there somewhere, not here.*

The doctor's forehead creased, glancing between them. *You girls are alone out there? When does he get back?*

She didn't like that line of questioning, not from a man she didn't know from anybody, not from a man who wasn't from around here. Not from anyone, really. She wished Lena was awake enough to divert with some other answer, wished this fancy doctor with his city-training could understand her, even going so far as to sign, *soon, just a few hours,* but of course he didn't understand.

His forehead creased and he started to say something, but Lena stirred. She moved to sit up, and Isa ran to help her even as the doctor was trying to get her to lie back down.

We really should take her to a hospital, he said, but Lena was already shaking her head.

No, we're going home, she said.

Isa didn't meet the doctor's gaze. She thought she agreed with him on that at least—that it wasn't a good idea to go home, that Lena needed a hospital—but she didn't argue, and they didn't give the doctor a chance to stop them on their way out.

. . .

The rot was spreading. Not in Lena's arm, thank God—Isa had seen to that—but it was spreading all the same, through the forest and through the tainted moonshine daddy was out selling all across town, none the wiser, and people would trace it back to the source. It wouldn't be long now, that was for certain.

. . .

Lena was sleeping off the blood loss and the drugs, or at least that's what she told Isa, but Isa couldn't trust anything she said anymore. All her life, everything her older sister had ever told her, Isa had known it was as good as fact—and not just because whatever she said was the honest truth.

That wasn't how the curse worked, though, was it?

Lena couldn't lie—that didn't mean everything she said was true, though.

And now, Isa didn't believe her. Not a word or a promise. She knew, deep in her soul—all the parts of her that had paid care to the old preacher's lessons on fire and brimstone, on hell and damnation, on all the bad things that happened to all the bad people who didn't repent and make right—knew, that there was no forgiveness for the thing she had done. Lena was alive, but there was a gulf between them, and in the darkness of the night, voices whispered: *why couldn't you just let me die?*

(They had the voice of her sister.)

Lena told her it wasn't her fault when her blackened arm was lying just beside her and she was half delirious, lying in a pool of her own blood. *Not your fault,* she said.

But just because Lena believed it didn't make it true.

Isa laid awake into the heavy quiet of the night and the crickets chirped a chorus and the voices whispered:

selfish, selfish, selfish, should've been you

▪ ▪ ▪

The morning came and with it worse things. Heavy, blanketing quiet that laid between them in a great divide. Lena barely noticed, drifting in a haze somewhere between dream and reality. She didn't even realize Isa though she resented her until the harsh crack of shotguns split the air and vibrated against the wood floors, making them both drop to the floor in fear and surprise. Isa insisted she be the one to look out and see what was going on.

She didn't realize that is might actually be true until she agreed to let her. And what kind of a person did that make her? What kind of sister?

Awful, probably, but her head pounded too steadily in time with the pulsing of her heart and the place where her arm should've been for her to figure it out for sure.

Isa peered up through the window over the counter, hunched so her head just barely peeked over the sill. She ran back to sit on the floor next to Lena.

Neighbors, she signed.

The neighbors are shooting at us? Lena asked. Maybe she was still dreaming. God, she hoped so. Let this be a terrible dream and let her wake up a better person who didn't resent her little sister for always needing more from her.

Isa nodded, and a shout filtered in from through the crack between the door and the frame: *Billy Larkin, we got a bone to pick with you. Get out here you sonofabitch.*

Lena waved at her sister. *Help me up,* she said.

She wrapped her good arm around Isa's neck and leaned against her. The world moved in waves and lurches around her as they moved toward the door. Isa helped her sister open it and walk out onto the porch.

They faced off against their friends and neighbors, still in last night's pajamas.

Can I help y'all with something? Lena called out at the group gathered out in their yard, hound dogs leashed at their sides and shotguns pointed down at the earth now that the girls were standing in front of them.

Where's your daddy, Lena? Mr. Jacobson asked.

We don't want no trouble, said Lena.

Bring your daddy out here and you won't get none, one of them hollered back.

Lena shared a glance with Isa. What would happen when they realized he wasn't here? Out here, neighbors looked out for each other, but there was an unspoken code of honor and to break it meant, well, backyard justice. And those same neighbors were its enforcers.

Veins of blackish rot dripped from the edges of some of their mouths—maybe Lena should've felt guilty for her part in that. All she could think was that they had all come here ready for a fight and daddy wasn't here—probably run off and left them until things smoothed over soon as he saw how this batch was corrupted.

And there was no telling what these people would do if they found out Billy Larkin wasn't here to face the brunt of their anger.

Lena felt Isa's fingers tighten against her waist in solidarity, and Lena just hoped she'd have time to go on resenting her sister for a little longer—and maybe forgive her sister and herself in good time, too.

Salvation came in a red pickup that threw up a line of dust down the drive and growled to a stop next to the crowd. The doctor swung open the door and asked, *Everything all right here?*

He took in the loose grips on leashes and the uneasy proximity of the guns and decided for his own self that no, in fact, everything was not all right. He reached back into the truck, grabbing his own shotgun, and pointed it at the ground near the neighbors' feet.

I think I'm gonna have to ask y'all to leave, he said flatly

I think I'm gonna ask you to mind your own business, one

of them retorted.

The doctor's lips twisted thin and flat as Lena watched him from the porch. *Not sure how the sheriff's gonna feel about this little militia gathering to threaten two teenage girls, but I'm thinking he might not like it—how about you?*

That seemed to grab their attention, and some of them shuffled like this might be more trouble than it was worth after all, but nobody made a move to leave.

A more explicit threat, then: the doctor cocked the shotgun at the crowd with a loud crack and said, *Get if you know what's good for you.*

He aimed the gun and stared them down until they started to shuffle off, but Lena could see in their eyes they'd come back soon as they thought they could get away with it.

The doctor waited until the yard was empty to walk over to the girls. *Are you okay?* he asked, examining them carefully, though from a distance.

Isa nodded and Lena asked, *Did you really call the sheriff?*

He shook his head no. *But it'll take them a while to figure that out. Long enough, anyway.*

Long enough for what? Isa signed, suspicious. Lena translated.

The doctor sighed heavily, setting his shotgun down against the porch railing and pushing a hand through his hair. *An explanation,* he said. *And an apology.*

What for?

For coming here today. And for thinking about not coming in the first place.

Lena was too dizzy and exhausted for riddles. She just stared at him straight-faced until he decided to continue, but he took his sweet time about it, that was for sure.

I don't know how—where to even start, he said. *I'm sorry. I guess that' where. I had to leave, had to, so I can't say I would do anything different, but I am sorry it meant leaving you girls.*

Lena squinted up at him, still stuck in that dream-like feeling where everything was almost possible, almost real. Was there something familiar there? She couldn't say she recognized him.

He rushed to fill the silence when neither of them said anything, and his voice was choked up thick with unshed tears. *Girls, girls, I'm so sorry. I've been gone so long, and you're half-grown without me here to help, and I never meant for it to be like this, but I hope you can forgive me, babies, I hope you can forgive me and let me help you now.*

Lena blinked and sat down heavily on the steps, the heady scent of honeysuckle strangling the breath right out of her. Her arm was missing and the doctor was crying, and she didn't know how to comfort her little sister for this thing she'd done to her and nothing felt real.

This, surely, was a dream, and she wasn't at all sure if it was a good one.

▪ ▪ ▪

Lena's arm slipped from around Isa's shoulder as she collapsed onto the porch steps, but Isa was almost too distracted to notice the missing weight of her sister leaning against her. She was staring at the doctor, birdseye focused, trying to line up the faces and make them fit.

They were different, and this one was lined older and happier than she had ever seen—but the broad strokes fit together in the way she remembered so well.

Mom? Isa signed, squinting at the man uncertainly.

He struggled over a swallow then nodded slowly.

Yeah, baby, it's me, he signed back, and Isa let out a sob. She ran and leapt into his arms at the bottom of the steps. He caught her and cradled her in his arms, though her legs almost dragged against the ground, too big as she was for this kind of thing.

This man was older than the mother she remembered, less soft, but still somehow the same.

Lena hung back, looking the doctor over suspiciously. *You left us,* she said, watching him with hard eyes.

He nodded slowly. *I did.* He didn't try to excuse it.

Isa nuzzled against his neck, inhaling the familiar garden scent of her mother now mixed with something more sterile and antiseptic, a new harsh, medical smell that hadn't been there before. She didn't mind it, though. Felt like it could grow to be its own kind of comforting.

It was the hardest thing I ever did, but I had to do it, he said. *And when I left, your daddy, he said he understood, but that if I left I wasn't to ever come back. Then I saw you girls the other day and—*

And you thought you could just come back here, that it would all be the same? Lena's voice was brittle carried on the air, even Isa could tell that just from looking at her.

Isa slipped down and glared at her sister. *Lena,* she signed, sharp and fast.

The silence and hurt still hung between them, and Isa's guilt pinched her neck like a vice, but this was their mother, this was the one person who had always loved them most, and she didn't really understand all of this any better than her sister did, but if their mother was back she going to make sure this time they got to keep him, anyhow and anyway.

Lena ignored her, not even looking over, though Isa knew she could understand her signs sidelong when she wanted. She stood and set a steady glare over Isa's head toward the doctor.

It's not okay, and we don't forgive you, Lena told the doctor.

Don't talk for me, Isa signed, moving right in front of her so she couldn't look away.

Lena let out a bitter laugh. *Are you forgetting,* she said. *I have to.*

Isa flinched at the words, hitting their mark wide and deadly like buckshot. She stepped back, away from her sister and toward her mother.

The doctor stepped forward to come between them in a distantly familiar way. *Girls,* he said, signing at the same time so Isa wouldn't miss it, but Lena wouldn't let him finish.

No, you don't get to decide to just show up like this! she said, her anger a flat and fragile thing. *You don't get to pretend you're some stranger and then show up and tell us we're special and you've always loved us and you didn't want to leave us. You just don't.*

The fury of her words leached the color from Lena's cheeks and she stumbled. Isa and the doctor both reached out at the same time, but Lena waved them off.

Don't—she said, but there wasn't as much fire behind it.

I'm sorry, the doctor said again. *I want to try to make it right if you'll let me.*

We will, Isa signed quickly. *We want to understand, we do—just—it might take some time.*

The doctor nodded, and Lena sat back down.

I know you'll need time—and explanations, and I understand that—but right now we need to get going before the neighbors come back.

What do you mean? Isa signed.

There's something wrong with them, some sickness spreading that's infecting them.

Somewhat against her will, Isa shared a furtive look with her sister, one their mother didn't miss.

What? he asked.

That might be because of us, Lena admitted, then glanced up at her sister and let out a deep sigh. *Because of me, really.*

He stayed quiet, waiting for them to finish.

I found a potion online—a cure, I guess—and it didn't go quite right, she told him. *It's what happened with—it's how I lost my arm.*

He nodded slowly. *Okay. I already saw two patients this morning,* the doctor—their mom, Isa was still trying to line those two disparate concepts up into one whole in her mind—said. *We need to get rid of the rest of it, destroy the evidence.*

We already did, said Lena. *It didn't work.*

No, I mean all of it. The still, everything.

It was Isa, not Lena, who reacted to that. *What, no, we can't. The still is too important, we can't just get rid of it!*

Harsh lines furrowed across their mother's brow. *That rotgut has only ever brought heartbreak to this family,* he said, a harshness like he well remembered.

Isa was still shaking her head, but Lena, who was pale and looked like she was drooping under the weight of her own body, said, *No, he's right, Isa.*

And when Isa ignored her, considered running up to the still to lay over it and protect it with her body as best she could, Lena pushed herself up to her feet and moved closer to sign, *He's right. We have to destroy it. All of it.*

Isa was staring hard into the stitching across the toes of her boots. Finally she looked up and nodded. *Okay, what do we do?*

They went inside. Their mother lingering awkwardly at the door as they grabbed the box of matches off the mantle and searched the cabinets in the kitchenette for lighter fluid, and when they couldn't find that, grabbed the leftover bottles of moonshine sitting on the counter and hauled it up the hill to douse the still with it, cranking up the furnace to make the fire burn even hotter.

Lena trailed a line of it back toward the house where she started dumping it all across the warped, wood flooring of the porch.

All of it, she said, eyes hard and shiny, as she continued pouring out the last of the liquor. Isa nodded and helped her.

They stood back from the house as their mother handed over the box of matches. Lena took one out and held it carefully between her fingers, the three of them silent as the moment stretched, considering this place that had, at times, been home to all of them, and, at times, been nothing but a house.

Lena swallowed and handed the match to Isa. *You do it,* she signed, and Isa understood it for the peace offering it was. She felt a deep pressure pushing up against the back of her eyes that she had to sniff away.

This flame was forgiveness. It was the end to a curse that never was, a curse that might always be.

Isa struck the head of the match against the matchbox, lighting it, but before she could toss it onto the porch, Lena grabbed her wrist.

Wait, she signed, running into the moonshine-drenched floors of the house.

The match had burned down almost to Isa's fingers by the time Lena returned, Isa's library books clutched to her chest with her good arm. Isa smiled, and, once she was clear, tossed the tiny flame onto the porch.

They moved up the driveway as the flames caught and spread, burning quickly across the alcohol soaked wood. The sisters stood beside their mother, watching the fire destroy the only home they'd ever known.

The fire burned hot and strong, deep red with orange tips—the color of death and bad moonshine. Dewdrops of sweat cooled against Isa's skin and the fire just kept burning, great waves of smoke reaching up toward the sky and coloring it gray until it blocked out the sunrise.

Lena swayed against Isa's side, and when she started to fall their mother caught her.

One look at her arm gave all the answer they needed. *Infection,* he explained, even though the swollen skin, pulled tight and red against the dark stitches was explanation enough.

Lena groaned weakly, and he was quick to scoop her up in his arms, carrying her like a baby even though she was mostly grown.

We need to get her to a hospital, he said, and Isa could see the fear fraying at the edges of his words—she felt it too.

Did she go through all of this, save her sister and risk her own soul, only to lose her now? A stranger of a mother wasn't enough to make up for that loss. If that was the trade being made, she'd gladly reverse it.

But, of course, that's not how things work—no more than potions cure ills or fairy tales can be trusted to teach anything at all.

They walked quickly toward the truck still parked in the driveway, Lena's head lolling against his sturdy arm, half-delirious with fever and shock. She mumbled something, and he shushed her, gently, but she persisted.

What baby? he asked.

The curse, she said, *will they be able to break it?*

He shared a frantic look with Isa, who was quite certain she hadn't misread the words on Lena's lips, mumbled as they were. Lena was dying from one cure and still hoping for some hope of another. Optimistic or stupid—maybe both at once.

The doctor clutched Lena closer. *Yes, baby, they will.*

And Isa could almost believe it.

[contributor bios]

Joe Aguirre writes from Shrewsbury, MA. He's driven a laundry truck, practiced maritime law, and sorted organs in a pathology lab. His work is forthcoming in *Fugue*.

Rachel Brittain is a writer from Arkansas. Her fiction has appeared or is forthcoming in *Hyperion and Theia, Parentheses Journal,* as the title story in *My Name Was Never Frankenstein*. When she isn't playing around in fictional worlds, she can be found writing for *Book Riot* and cuddling animals.

Charles Conley has received fellowships from the Fine Arts Work Center, Teachers & Writers Collaborative, and the Sozopol Fiction Seminars. His stories and essays have been published in *North American Review, Harvard Review, Southern Review, Fiction Writers Review,* and *Teachers & Writers Magazine*. His MFA in fiction is from the University of Minnesota, and he lives in Minneapolis.

Alison Foster is the former Dean of Students at the Calhoun School in New York City. After a year in Washington, DC, she is back living in an old schoolhouse on the Lower East Side. She is taking classes at Gotham Writers and working on memoir and a murder mystery.

[contributor bios]

Caroljean Gavin's work has appeared in *The Ampersand Review, Voicemail Poems, Eckleburg,* and the 2011 *Press 53 Open Awards Anthology*. Currently she is working on a story collection, a novel, finding a library job, and raising her two boys to be amazing and kind.

Debbie Graber's fiction has appeared in *Cagibi, Electric Literature, Harper's,* and *Zyzzyva,* among other journals. Her story collection, *Kevin Kramer Starts on Monday,* was published in 2016 by Unnamed Press.

Originally from Western New York, **Jasmine Sawers** now lives and pets dogs outside St. Louis. Her work has appeared in such publications as *Ploughshares, Fairy Tale Review,* and *[PANK]*. She is a proud Kundiman fellow and graduate of the MFA program at Indiana University.

Jenny Wu teaches fiction writing at Washington University in St. Louis. She is the 2018-2019 WashU Senior Fiction Fellow and was the 2016 Humanities Honors Fellow at the Bill & Carol Fox Center for Humanistic Inquiry. Her stories can be found in *The Literary Review, The Collagist, wildness, Hobart,* and others.

CPSIA information can be obtained
at www.ICGtesting.com
Printed in the USA
BVHW032033200920
589230BV00031B/111